HøneyRider

BenjaminNorthSpence

aNovel

— NORTHERNPROS BOOKS —

HØNEY RIDER ː A NØVEL
COPYRIGHT © 2013 BENJAMIN NORTH SPENCER

NorthernPros Books is a division of NorthernPros Creations, an independent publishing organization responsible for multiple print and online texts.

HØNEY RIDER : A NØVEL is available online at
ShallowMidwestBlues.Tumblr.com.
where the entire text of the story is has been randomized.

FIRST EDITION | FIRST PRINTING
ISBN$_{13}$ 978-0-9794980-3-9
ISBN$_{10}$ 0979498031

ACKNOWLEDGMENTS FROM THE AUTHOR

I would like to extend my appreciation and thanks to:
Nadine, Karen, Michael & Cathy, Sunday & Christian, Kim, Kerry, Frank & Val,
Sterz & Calder, Buff, Pete, Barile, Genevieve, & Chaz ...
you know what you mean to me ...

Høney Rider is based on actual events ... however ... the content, characters, and storyline have been changed enough to warrant the use and application of the term NØVEL.

FOR KE & JPL

WAKING

1 ... When I close my eyes I see James reaching for me, for anything to hold on to. Behind him, there's only the cool autumn air and the flat gunmetal gray of the Erie Canal. The horror restarts. It never completes. There is no sound. No splash. No body. It's as if it never happened, if only for the lack of proof.

2 ... I remember standing in the front room of my childhood home on Mount Hope Avenue, the limbs of the large oak tree in the front yard swaying in the wind. Rain was pelting the window. Dad was frantic that morning, talking to himself, shoving knick-knacks around the drawer where all our random objects end. "Tip?" he said. "Do you know where that *thing* is?" I asked him what he was going to do without me. Dad stopped. He said, "I'll manage. But that doesn't mean I won't miss you."

3 … Morning again. Someone kissed my forehead. I could hear whispers coming from the hallway. I recognized one of the voices. It was Dad. He was telling one of the nurses something. She said, "Go home. You need sleep too. I'll keep an eye on Henry." I waited for them to leave before I opened my eyes. I don't need the attention. I don't need the questions. I have another monochromatic autumn to keep me company.

4 … I woke from a dream with a kick. Dad was telling me a story. "Do you remember?" he said. I was watching his lips through the hole in his beard. He said, "The house was condemned when I saw her listing in the public auction. She was just an address then, a sad story. I knew the neighborhood and the house. I went to the historical society to examine the plat books. She had been abandoned for years. When I was finally able to get inside, I realized the extent of the damage. It was heartbreaking. But she was everything I wanted. The stone work, the craftsmanship, the leaded windows, a yard for you and your sister. Your mom was pregnant with you. Until then, we'd been living in small apartments. I wanted a home for us. I know there's a lot of work to be done …." He laughed. "I've been saying that for twenty years. I guess I never saw the need to change much after your mom and I separated and you kids moved away. Now that you're living in Iowa … who knows what will happen?" I offered little response. I don't remember the house he was talking about. I can't imagine what it looks like or where it is. I'm sure I should. I'm preoccupied. If I so much as wiggle an eyebrow I can feel the stitches in the back of my head, the new scar forming. It was easier to fade into the list of objects Dad found in the walls of the house over the years. I know that he's trying to stir my memories, but the images don't match the cards he's turning over. The one thing I do remember is waiting for James at a diner. It was the night he got stabbed. I was trying to convince him to go to the hospital, but James had other plans.

5 … An old man rolled a cart of magazines and books into the room today. I reached for *A Portrait of the Artist as a Young Man*, but the old man stopped me. "That one's reserved for another patient. It has the pink tag." I selected a History of Rochester instead. When it comes to my birthplace or its politics I'm as ignorant as a tourist. The things I know are less large. For instance, I don't think of the Erie Canal as the eighth wonder of the world. When I think of the Erie Canal, I remember Honey leaping from the High Point, holding her shirt and her nose as she splashed into the shimmering water. It was summer. We were younger. But how can I be sure? *Honey Rider* is only a name to me. Like the ghost in the chair beside me, every time I reach out, she vanishes. I know I shouldn't fall asleep, but someone whispers, "It's time to dream again."

6 … The nurses woke me briefly. They were lifting me, rolling me, changing my bedding. I messed myself. "This is normal," one of them said.

7 … Jasper is my roommate. He's in traction, bandaged from head to toe, and he sleeps with his eyes open. Its unnerving, but what choice does he have? He doesn't have any eyelids. He barely has any skin at all. He burned it off in a fire he started while getting high on gasoline. His speech is almost inaudible. His lips, mouth and throat were liquefied in the blaze.

Jasper grunted in my direction, "Stop." He took a long deliberate breath and continued, "That." I stopped typing. Jasper sighed. "Thank you," he said.

8 … Dad woke me with whispers, more snapshots of my time line. His words are sensations, colors, and sounds. Time is a series of bubbles. In one of them, I can see Dad's hand. He is holding my hand, and leading me through the snow toward a house. I can feel the texture of extra yarn inside one of my mittens. I bite the end of the thumb sleeve. The color of the mittens is a forgery. Perhaps so is the memory of Dad leading me up the front steps as the family entered the old house on Mount Hope Avenue for the first time. Maybe this is all just a personal poetics, a chance to buy back those spent opportunities. The trouble is knowing that some things, once done, cannot be undone. This is a realization I wish I did not have.

9 … Memories arrive like new snow. At first, they melt. Then they begin to accumulate. The horizon is bright white. The most uncomfortable moments of my life are filling in the landscape. In one unfortunate pause, I relive a catalyst. I watch Mom's second husband force his hand over her mouth. She tries to fend him off, but she can't. She's not strong enough. He plummets into her as I storm into the room. I want to stop the rape but he is stronger than both of us. He lands blow after blow, alternating his strikes between Mom and I. In one lucky moment, I land a startling blow of my own. He is stunned. Mom is stunned. He turns his attention to me and me alone, beating me into a pile in the corner before dragging me down the stairs and out onto the lawn. He calls me, "Little fucker" and lets

me go. I run until I can't run anymore, hiding in the shadows. It's raining light. The entire neighborhood is in aura. Somewhere on Culver Road I have a seizure. When I come to, I'm at a dimly lit strip mall. There's a pay phone. I pick up the receiver and try to remember a phone number. Dad answers and says, "I'll be right there."

10 ... Living with Dad wasn't easy. It wasn't him, it was me. I had post-traumatic stress from the years I'd been living with Mom and her second husband. I was on high alert. Dad was encouraging me to come down from the ceiling, but I couldn't release my grip. Eventually, he stopped trying so hard. He just continued caring, making himself available. Dad offered a gentler side to things. He gave me the time and space I needed to heal, to breathe, to feel safe. Behind the house is the Mount Hope Cemetery. Between the cemetery and the house was an old cherry tree where I liked to read. In one summer, I read half of Dad's collection. But for all the words and keys I had been handed, none had succeeded in cutting through the layers of anger and frustration that cocooned me. It was a phone call from Prudence, my older sister, that finally succeeded in handing me a knife. I answered the telephone. Prudence said, "Hey fatty! I need a favor." There was a box in the attic. Her birth certificate was in there somewhere. I hung up with her and went upstairs to look. The paint-worn wood stairs to the attic were sprinkled with plump dead flies. The layers of plaster on the walls were cracked. The box Prudence described was in a corner near Dad's old clothes. I found her birth certificate and some photos and a note-book. *Poems by Prudence Nighteen* was written on the cover. I turned the pages. There were poems about her emotions and boys and stuff I thought I could eventually tease her about. I tucked the notebook under my arm and called Prudence to let her know I had found the certificate and spent the rest of the afternoon in the cherry tree reading her notebook. Each poem seemed worse than the one before it. There were scores of poems inspired by the letters of words and names. I was appalled and amazed that she would share her feelings this way. It was terribly unguarded. One

of the things she had written started with the letters B-R-O-T-H-E-R. It was silly, but I was touched that Prudence had included me in her book of stupid poems.

11 ... Sometime later, my English teacher gave the class a poetry assignment. I planned to use one of Prudence's poems. That night I flipped through the pages looking for something halfway decent. When I found it, I copied it in my own handwriting and turned it in the next day. The following week, my teacher called the class to attention and said she had a winner for the poetry assignment. Little did anyone know she was creating a contest out of it. "I reviewed all of your pieces and though some of your poems were well written, one of you really opened yourself up to the possibilities of what poetry can be. Henry," she said. "Good job." My classmates were in awe. I was a freak to them, a creep, the epileptic who probably should have been in the "special" classes down the hall. I didn't even remember what poem I copied down. Only after school, on the bus, did I re-read Prudence's poem. It was about our parents' divorce, how she felt like a pencil filling in the spaces, then flipping around and erasing it all. There was never anything real on the page – "only the impression that the family might have meant something to someone, sometime." It was well written. I was very proud of myself.

12 ... I'm feeling better. The doctor said I can go home soon. Things are coming more easily now. I've been thinking a lot about the writing. At my high school graduation, my English teacher mentioned something about my poem to Dad. Dad said, "I had no idea. Have you been writing a lot?

Writing can be a lucrative career." I didn't want a career. I wanted the pain of Life to go away. I wanted to be free of the past. That summer, I took a job at a restaurant washing dishes and making salads. It wasn't glamorous. It was money, enough to keep me significantly stoned and numb. That fall, I started at the Rochester Institute of Technology, Dad's Alma Mater. I had no interest in college but it was a free education. Dad worked as a photographer at the school and all employees' families received free tuition. While taking my general education requirements I filled in my schedule with an English literature class taught by the poet Jaja Paduzzi. On the first day of class, Jaja stormed into the classroom in rubber boots, slammed down a stack of books and shoved a smile into the side of his face. He said, "It doesn't matter what you learn, as long as I teach!" That semester, after reading a few of my poems, Jaja turned me onto Walt Whitman, e.e. Cummings, Langston Hughes, Frank O'Hara, Allen Ginsberg, and the Beats. It was at R.I.T, under Jaja's tutelage that writing became an important part of each day. I would reach for my pen to understand and to elude myself. If I was unhappy, I would write. If I wanted to get laid, I wrote. When I left a note for Dad or wrote a shopping list, I would do it in a poem. It was saccharine, but I was happy doing it. I was happy. I had a purpose. Or so I thought.

13 ... Those days, I took most of what Jaja said to heart. One day, he invited me to his office and said, "You should get out of here. There's no poetry program at R.I.T.. You need a good program ... You ever heard of the Writers Workshop in Iowa?" I didn't even know where Iowa was. I had never been out of the state – except to visit my relatives in Ohio. I submitted an application anyway. I didn't tell a soul. When I received the acceptance letter in the mail, it was as if I caught the bird on the windowsill. I found a little cage for it and kept it like a secret.

14 ... Dad and I were solid. The trip to Iowa was our finest moment. We bonded, forever entangled in the confusion that was letting go. Now, I'm not sure we're so buddy-buddy. He was in a knot this morning when the hospital released me. Thankfully, Jasper was being goofy. The doctors have him on a new pain medicine. He said, "It's strong. Real strong."

15 ... I was signing my release forms when the sheriffs deputies arrived to talk with Jasper. Dad rolled me out of the room in a wheelchair. Jasper gargled, "I'll miss you" and I gave him the finger. Then one of the sheriffs closed the door. Dad was keeping to himself. When we got to the lobby, he locked the wheels on my wheelchair and said, "I'll bring the car around." The lobby windows overlook the main entrance to the hospital. Across the street from the main entrance is the cemetery where I hit my head one week ago today. I don't remember it, but I know it happened. I have the damages to prove it.

WALKING

16 ... There is no way around it. The Mount Hope Cemetery borders the hospital and surrounds the house. Dad did his best to take the long way, along the river. He drove through Highland Park, around the reservoir where the annual Lilac Festival is held, and stopped. "Do you remember that cannon," he asked. There was a long bronze cannon in a field. There are children playing on it. I shake my head, *No*. Dad said, "You and Prudence used to play on it." It's as if I'm hearing a lot of things for the first time. Inevitably, we arrived at the house, on the North East corner of the cemetery. It's a blur, but I know Honey is dead. I know that she's buried in my own back yard. I want to tell Dad how disturbed I am, but there is an aura of white and red ribbons. I have to get inside and lie down. I don't want another seizure, not now. Not after I've come this far.

17 ... Time is written. Time is erased.

18 ... In his book *Writing Your Memoir*, Samuel Kim suggests using a timer when you write. It forces you to write something specific within an arbitrary time frame. He poses the question, "What can you write in an hour?" The question is, when you're at the crossroads of sanity, how many words can you take in the wrong direction before turning back becomes impossible?

19 … My second night back in the house. Dad and I had a quiet dinner. He's trying to stay positive, but he's struggling. In addition to Honey's death and my set back, he's got a lot on his mind. Work is slow. Some of his colleagues have been laid off. He hasn't been sleeping. Before heading into his room for the night, he asks if I remember how to make the milk? "I can't make it the way you do," he adds. Dad went upstairs while I warmed some milk with a pinch of nutmeg, a pinch of cinnamon, and a shot of brandy. While the milk steeped, I went down to the basement to look for the canister of grass I remember stashing. It took a minute, but I found it. I rolled a joint on the clothes dryer. Something smelled to high heaven. I put the joint behind my ear and opened the clothes washer. There was a ring of moldy towels in the wash bin. I used a stick to breakup the ring and restarted the wash, adding more detergent than may have been necessary. When the milk was ready, I brought a mug of it to Dad. He was already asleep. I set the milk on his bedside table and navigated the noisy floorboards, the squeaky staircase, the immense front door with the loose windowpane, and smoked the joint on the front porch, counting fireflies. When the fireflies retired, I tried to think about Honey.

20 … I was right. I do have the first note Honey ever passed me. Until that morning, we had made eye contact on the school bus and in the halls, but Honey was just one of hundreds of other girls at the school, just another set of boobs, another great ass, another pair of calves. She took the seat across the aisle from me in American History. She knew me but didn't know me. She said, "Hi." I said, "Hi." She passed me the note a few minutes later. Honey wrote "Stop staring at me." I didn't realize I had been. I wrote a "?" and handed the note back to her. Honey spent time on her response. What she handed back to me was a sketch of the classroom. There's a staggered line between Mr. Mifflin's eyes and Honey's legs. I looked at Honey. I watched Mr. Mifflin. He stole a glance at something in Honey's immediate personal vicinity and licked his lips. When he turned to write something on the chalkboard, Honey spun around to see my reac-

tion. It was disturbing. I wanted to pound him.

21 … Passing notes became a regular thing for Honey and I. As you might expect, my feelings for her grew. The more I paid attention, the more beautiful she became. The notes were easy for me. I didn't have to stand up straight or say anything clever. I could deliberate until I had something good to share. I was thinking to the point of hesitation. Honey wasn't over thinking things. After school one day – I had detention, she was going home on the bus – Honey handed me a note and said, "Call me?" I never made detention. I stared at the piece of paper and the loops in Honey's phone number until I had a small seizure. Then I walked it off on one of the practice fields.

22 … Honey called me before I could work up the nerve to call her. I can't remember what we talked about, but that call led to other calls, and other exchanges. Eventually, we learned each other's daily schedules. We ate lunch together in the cafeteria. We snuck cigarettes at the gazebo on the edge of the lacrosse field. It was Honey who asked me out first. She said, "We should get an ice cream or something sometime." When the unofficial *date* came, I rode my bicycle to her large gray house on Edgerton Street, in the Cobbs Hill neighborhood. We walked to the top of Cobbs Hill and around the reservoir to where the ice cream stand was. I remember the deep green rolling hills of trees and the city stretched out below us. Honey ate her ice cream then fed the cone, in pieces, to the waterfowl at the edge of the reservoir. It was warm that day and when we sat down in the grass, the way she crossed her legs, I caught a glimpse of her inner thighs. I took a deep breath and choked on a chocolate chip. When I recovered, I felt

something in my teeth. My insecurities were in high tide. I froze. Why was this unbeatable chick there with me? I had zits for Christ's sake. I was paranoid that she was looking at my zits. It was uncomfortable. She felt it too. After several long awkward silences, she said, "You're being weird."

23 … Honey was never part of a clique like most people at school. She kept to herself a lot of the time. On our ice cream date, Honey wanted to believe that I could be her friend. But all I could think about was fucking her. It was no use trying to weed out the feelings I had for her. The seed was planted. I convinced myself that Honey wasn't interested in me. And if she wasn't interested in me then I wasn't going to waste my time being interested in her. After a while we stopped calling each other, we stopped writing notes in class, we even ignored each other in the halls. I stopped looking for her, and eventually, Honey disappeared completely.

24 … My fingers and hands are getting more nimble. An hour of writing isn't as difficult as it was even a few days ago. The stitches came out on their own last night. I found them on my pillow this morning. I suppose it's not that important, I just love pounding on these keys.

25 … Mom came to Dad's house from Church. She was wearing a blue

dress with a broad white collar. Her hair was teased. She was wearing a lot of make-up, a lot of perfume. Dad let me answer the door. We stayed on the front porch. We hugged, she was gentle, but firm. She rubbed my head and asked me how I was feeling. Speaking is still too difficult. Writing in the notebook is easier. "Better," she read. She reached for the pen and notebook to write another question. I brushed her hand away and wrote, "You can speak, Ma. I can hear you just fine." Our conversation was all small-talk. I had the luxury of time but I'm not one to indulge a leisurely outlook on things. Time is of the essence and I still have questions about what happened. I wrote one of those questions in the notebook and showed it to her. "Who is James?"

26 ... Mom said, "I was there when you two met." Mom and I were shopping for a Halloween costume at the thrift store up the street from where we lived on Hazelwood Terrace. I was eight or nine years old. She was showing me lengths of cloth for a cape when someone inside one of the clothes racks poked me with a stick. When I looked inside the clothes rack James poked me in the face. It hurt and it made me cry. Mom put me in the cart and chased James through the store. She found him hiding behind a woman she recognized. They were our new neighbors. A few days later, Mom sent me down the street to play with James. I remembered this part. I didn't want to play with him. What if he poked me in the face again? I refused. Mom ordered me to go. She said, "He's new here. He doesn't have any friends." Even at that tender age, I understood why. He was a jerk. I walked toward James' house, but I didn't go into the yard. I sat down on the curb across the street. James was in the driveway, riding a BMX bike. When he saw me, he rode away. I was glad. But then he turned around in the street and rode back toward me ... fast. I expected him to be a jerk again, but he turned into the driveway of one of the houses and popped off of the transition of the driveway rising high above the sidewalk and the lawn before redirecting himself in mid-air toward the slope of the front yard. It was something you'd see at a BMX contest. In the next driveway, James lifted up on his handlebars and was airborne again. At the height of

the lift, James leveled out, his cheeks swollen with air, his face as red as my Superman cape. He soared over the steps and the sidewalk and most of the front lawn. As he touched down in the Cavagnero's lawn his rear wheel clipped an irrigation pipe. The bike stopped and James flipped over the handlebars and rolled into the street, skidding on his chin and shoulder until he stopped. He stood up and picked the gravel from the palms of his hands, flicking it back into the street. It was probably one of the coolest crashes I'd ever seen. James saw me as he examined the gash in his hand. It was bloody, awesome.

27 … It took a fight in Boy Scouts to bind me and James completely. A few of the neighborhood kids and one of their Dad's started their own troop at a church up the street. They met once a week. Mom and her second husband thought it would be a good idea if I joined. It sounded fun enough, but this was a city Boy Scout troop. What we lacked in fresh air and Nature, we made up for in cement. The night of my first meeting, I showed up with a new uniform. Mom had pressed my clothes to have creases. I looked like a jackass. Some of the kids in my troop identified me as an easy target, and they took an opportunity during a game of *Shoot'm Up Bust'm Up* in the church yard to make an example out of me. The way *Shoot'm Up Bust'm Up* worked, one team would throw a football to the other team. Whoever caught the ball would try to get to the opponent's end zone without being tackled. The other team threw the ball directly to me. I ran into the end zone without getting tackled, once. The next time the ball came to me I got a bloody fat lip. The third time, I got tackled into the dirt. James was watching from across the street. He wasn't in the Boy Scouts. He was free to do what he wanted. He watched me get leveled several times before he asked if he could play on my team. The troop agreed. James didn't look like much of a threat. They thought they could pummel him too. But what James lacked in size, he made up for in sadism. One down after another, he knocked the crap out of the kids in my Boy Scout troop. Eventually they didn't want to play anymore. Now that I think about it, anyone who ever put James in their sights inevitably lost.

28 … James and I became inseparable. We were young and dumb. We liked the things our parents told us to stay away from – fire, breaking things, graffiti, fighting, girls, smoking, drugs, and stealing – then lying to them about where we'd been and what we'd been doing. In ninth grade, James transferred from his public school to my private school. We met every morning in front of the laundromat up the street. I would bring white bread toast and a mix of coffee and hot chocolate. James would bring a few cigarettes. We would eat and smoke before playing arcade games until the quarters ran out or we absolutely had to get to school. We saw each other throughout the day in the halls, but James was in the remedial classes and all of those classes were in the basement. After school, there were several hours where we could do what we wanted to do. We were almost always together until dinner, but we never – and I mean never – hung out at his house. Eventually, I began to piece things together. His family sucked, like my family sucked. We were reflections of one another. We leaned on each other for support. One night, while I was trying to focus on my homework, James tapped at my bedroom window. He was wearing his mother's sunglasses. It was dark. He took off the sunglasses when he climbed in. The his left eye was blood red and swollen. His father had beaten him because, as James put it, "the lima beans were too salty." James gave me a look and said, "Wait, what happened to you?" I had a similar dinner experience. Mom's second husband asked me for the butter knife during dinner. I was going through knife training in Boy Scouts at the time. The organization teaches that when handing a knife to someone, it is important to wait for them to acknowledge that they have it securely in their grip before releasing it. I tried this at dinner with the butter knife. Mom's second husband wasn't in the mood. He had me on the floor against the cupboard with my throat in his grip before I could explain. When he stopped hitting me, he wiped his mouth with a napkin and threw it at me. Then he picked up the butter knife, sat down at the head of the table and buttered his bread. Mom was frozen with fear and so ashamed that she couldn't look up from her plate. How anyone could live

like that is beyond me ... now. Yet, there we all were. Trapped in patterns that needed breaking.

29 ... Another day. James called the house and asked me to come over. He wanted to show me something. It was an invitation I couldn't refuse. The house was modest, well-kept, quiet, not at all the picture of chaos that I had imagined. There were doilies on almost every flat surface, pictures of people I'd never met on the mantle over the fireplace, a small piano in the corner of the living room and the faint scent of pipe smoke. James said I should follow him. He had a wad of keys and unlocked a door in the hall-way that led to the basement. At the bottom of the stairs was another door, he unlocked it. James said, "My dad would kill us if he knew we were in here." James got the door open and disappeared into the darkness. The light came on. It was a bunker of guns, knives and swords, and stacks of ammunition boxes with Property of the U.S. ARMY stenciled on the sides. On the walls were photos of men in fatigues, men in battle, photos of James' dad and his Army buddies sitting atop a tank. There was a helmet with a hole in it hanging on the wall. James was handling a grenade. He tossed it to me and I caught it. "Relax, it's a lighter. What do you think?" he asked. I said, "It's excessive." James took the grenade lighter and lead me out. We went back upstairs, to the second floor. His parents' room had flower curtains, wood furniture and separate beds. James' room was down the hall. It looked like a jail cell or a bunker. He set the grenade lighter on a black trunk under a row of windows and walked into the middle of the room. His bed was small, the sheets were perfectly tucked. His walls were blank, but for one small poster of Harry Houdini. There were no dirty dishes, or clothes lying around. There really wasn't much to see. James folded his arms and smiled, and quietly pointed under his bed. I leaned down and lifted the edge of the bed cover. There, in nothing but Army-issued underwear and a soldier's helmet, pointing the barrel of a rifle at my face, sweating and mumbling, was James' father. The long barrel was a blur, his stare focused someplace off in the distance. He grunted and pulled the trigger, twice. After a third click, he whined and backed into the

shadows. We were both freaked out, but James was red with laughter. "I wish you could see your face right now."

30 ... One night James' mother burned dinner and his father "scolded her" with a rolling pin. When James came home, he found his mother unconscious on the living room floor between his father and the Tv. James said, "I guess I finally snapped. I beat him for the next hour or so. The neighbors called the cops. They think I beat my mom too. You know better, but she won't even back me up. My own mother is throwing me under a bus." James was telling me all of this outside the courthouse, after his hearing two days later. "The house was filling with gas when the cops got there. I saw those loopy *auroras* you always talk about when you have a seizure?" I reminded him that they were called *auras*. He said, "Whatever you call them ... You were kind of there, in a way." I asked him what he was going to do if the police hadn't shown up when they did. "I was going to burn the place to the ground," he said. Something had changed in him. He wasn't angry, he was mad. An officer guided James to an unmarked transport car and guided him into the back seat. James was going away for a while.

31 ... James was sent to a detention center on the other side of the city. When he got out, he moved into an apartment with some real rough characters. He started using cocaine. Then he started stealing to support the habit. When we did get together, James was always amped. If he wasn't high he was trying to score. One night – shortly after I moved into Dad's house – James showed up in *an old friend's* new Cadillac. He was in a good mood, on his way to feed someone's cat. He had been watching

their house. James asked me to go with him, "You've got to check this place out." When we got there, James found the key under the mat and we went in. He started calling for "Muffy!" I felt like I'd just walked into a magazine. There wasn't a lampshade out of place. Everything was new and/or very old. James was going in and out of doors and rooms, calling for "Muffy." He said, "I'll check upstairs." He went up while I admired the place. James came down a few minutes later. He said, "She's upstairs, sleeping. Want to go?" I was eating a yogurt in the kitchen. I asked him if I could finish the yogurt. He said, "Bring it with you." I guess I should have suspected something, but I trusted him. Maybe he was there to feed a cat I never saw. One thing's for sure, the house was all over the news a few days later. The anchor said a "cat burglar" had gotten away with over $100,000 in jewelry while the family was on vacation in the Bahamas. The hard part wasn't suspecting that I had been there when it happened, or that my fingerprints were probably now on file at the police station. It was difficult realizing that James never believed in limits – even when it came to our friendship. I didn't want to be involved in risks like that. Especially if I wasn't getting some of the take.

32 ... Raine was the new kid at school and he frustrated the hell out of me. Trigonometry made sense to him. It bothered me that he was smart, that I wasn't, but we rode the same bus to and from school, so we had four hours each day to get to know each other. It was the same bus that Honey took. Raine and Honey had known each other since they were kids. They lived one block over from each other. Raine's father split when he was young. He was raised by his deaf mother and ailing grandmother, and in many ways Honey's parents. He was smart, funny, and likable. His only real weakness was that he loved being high.

33 … Raine worked a steady job to legitimize his primary source of income of brokering large quantities of marijuana. James and I were regular customers. One afternoon, James and I met Raine at Zab's, a hot dog and burger joint where he worked. He had a pound of *Kush* waiting for us. Raine locked the door and we went to the walk-in cooler to see and taste the Kush. Raine had fashioned a carrot into a bowl and had already packed it. Raine said, "This strain is last year's Cannabis Cup winner." The high was slow and long and broad. Raine packed a second bowl and James stepped out to use the bathroom. When he came back the bowl was empty. James said he'd had "plenty." There was an exchange of money and James and I went somewhere to weigh out the orders. We stood to make a few thousand dollars each and get stoned for weeks. It was a great set up. A couple days later, Raine got fired from Zab's. He said there was two-thousand bucks missing from the register the day we picked up the Kush. He couldn't understand it. But I did. When I asked James about it, he denied the allegation with a cold indifference. He said, "I wouldn't do that to a friend." I could read between the lines. He never considered Raine a friend.

34 … Daily habit: When going to sleep for the night, organize what you're going to write about when you wake. Wake early. Write until you are finished. Refuse interruption. Do not make excuses.

35 … I was looking through my old notebooks today. In one of them, there is a drawing of a bridge spanning a lush valley. Under the concrete arches

of the bridge are stacks of giant cages of rocks. I know this place. I have been there. I just can't remember when.

36 ... James finished rolling a joint and lit it. We were at School 1, overlooking the highway, sitting on those springy animals. He said, "I met that girl you keep talking about. Honey? She asked me if I wanted to go camping with her this weekend." He paused to take a drag off the joint, then held it in. I was dumbfounded. "Are you going?" I asked. "You're not much of a camper." James passed me the joint and said, "And I don't want to get locked in some tent in the woods with a chick I barely know." I asked him why he thought he'd be in such an intimate setting with the girl I let get away. "Oh, shit! You like her!? I won't go if you don't want me to go," he said. I didn't know what I wanted him to do, but I knew that nothing good would come of it. James laughed and blew smoke in my face. "She's just a girl, *H*. She's just a girl. Besides, what about that Myra chick?"

37 ... Myra was way out of my league, beyond beautiful, and brilliant. When we met, she was sitting on a stool at the end of the long counter at a cafe in Pittsford. Dad was chatting her up as he paid for our breakfast. He and I had come out to the suburbs that morning to rent bicycles to ride along the Erie Canal path. Dad wore his spandex so (even at five miles an hour) he could be more aerodynamic. I was completely embarrassed. I tried to laugh it off and get him out of there, but I couldn't take my eyes off Myra. She was half-Asian, graceful and patient, and a little curious why Dad decided to pick on her. As Dad and I left the cafe, Myra and I met eyes. I went back to the counter to apologize for Dad's behav-

ior. I said, "He just goes for it … I'm sorry … But, um, do you want to get together some time?" Her face turned plum-red as she realized by the paused expressions of the waiters, busboys and customers that they'd all heard my awkward proposal. I think she agreed just to get me out of there. I don't think she ever really expected to start anything, but it did. The relationship, if you could call it that, was a real slow mover. Everything felt plotted. Myra was older than me, better put together. She liked to take things slow. At that time she was studying piano at the Eastman School of Music. She lived in one of the new turnkey apartments at Liberty Pole Plaza. It was a mecca of modernity and comfort. The apartment itself was evidence enough that we were from two very different worlds. Everything was digital and voice controlled. If she was out of milk, Myra would say, "Refrigerator" and the refrigerator would answer her. "Grocery list. Add milk." The refrigerator added the milk to a printable grocery list. She had a robot vacuum that turned on at noon everyday and cleaned the floors of the apartment. An assistant came once a week to clean and shop for groceries. Myra wanted for nothing. Because of this, she was peaceful. The only struggle in her life was how to play her instrument better. I remember Myra sitting at the baby grand piano in her living room, gently improvising as the sun went down and I set the ant blotter acid on her tongue. I remember the way she growled at me. Myra said, *This* is going to be fun!"

38 … I led Myra around the apartment with my voice as we peaked. She was wearing a blindfold, laughing whenever she bumped into a wall or a piece of furniture. I coaxed her into her bedroom, to the edge of her bed. Myra giggled. "I know where we are." I helped Myra lay down and unbuttoned her shirt, exposing her belly. I kissed around her belly button. She said, "I know where this is going." I asked her if she liked pain. "Maybe I don't know where this is going. What kind of pain?" she asked. "Candle wax," I said. "I could be persuaded," she answered. I untied her pants and dripped a little candle wax south of her belly button. She winced and relaxed. I was admiring the tightness of her skin, her jaw line, her neck and shoulders, her slender arms and talented fingers. Myra was laughing, "I

like acid," she said. "It feels good." Good acid can be a kind of master key in a hallway of doors. For Myra, the ant blotter acid led her to a realization that began with the story of her parent's death. "I had no idea," I said, setting the candle on her night stand. "You never asked," she added, taking off her blindfold. Myra continued. Her parents were leaving the opera when a drunk driver lost control of his car and drove onto the sidewalk where they were walking. They both died because of their injuries, first Myra's father, then her mother. They were apparently rich to begin with, but the insurance and the lawsuit made it so Myra was wealthy. Because of this financial freedom, she felt obligated to live a life that honored her parents' wishes. That meant focusing on her music. She liked me, but would never love me. We were just too different. Myra said, "This will be the last time we see each other," and then she removed the rest of her clothes. "Let's make the best of it."

39 ... Honey called to ask if I wanted to trip on Friday night. Her folks were taking their sailboat to Canada for the weekend. "The house will be all ours," Honey said. It would be her and James, Raine and Alise, Lynnae and Ransom, and me. "It's got ants on it," Honey said. "James said you tried it already?" It was happy acid, I told her. "It's a *Rider*," I said, "I'm in." When Friday night rolled around, we gathered at Honey's dining room table and divided the ants among us. Honey and James took theirs. Raine and Alise shared two. Lynnae fed hers to Ransom and he fed his to her. I took two. The next several hours were filled with music, abandoned board games, and a round of hide-and-seek that lasted an eternity because James and I climbed onto the top of the house and smoked a joint that shifted the trip into overdrive. Everyone thought we had walked off somewhere. We were only discovered when a laughing fit overtook us. Honey had to walk into the street to see us. When she did, she shrieked with excitement. It was a good batch of acid, a real *Rider*. *Riders* have a velocity and a power about them. If you can control it, the *Rider* will take you over the horizon and bring you back again. The *Rider* does the work, all you have to do is hang on.

40 … James and I arrived at Honey's with our bathing suits and a quarter ounce of the Kush. Honey had another batch of acid. It was a four-square of blue blotter with a rainbow circle at the center. We each took one hit and divided the fourth. James rolled a blunt of the Kush and we were off … Flash forward several hours … I came out of the foggy acid haze as James and I leapt off the garage roof into Honey's pool. The weightlessness was frightening. I could feel the cold grasp of gravity claim us as we fell through the air. I can imagine the plunge, but I don't remember it. The splash triggered time travel and I found myself lying on Honey's living room floor beside James, wearing only our towels. (What takes place in these empty spaces is what makes acid unique. The mind can create dreamscapes that deliver a prolonged shift in consciousness. There are moments when the senses are so swollen that deep meaning can be derived from the tip of a sewing pin. Acid also has its downs. These are called *swells*. *Swells* have the potential for fun, but they are largely the sign of an unstable chemistry.) James and I stared at the living room ceiling as we dried off. He was looking at the chandelier. I was focusing on the architecture of the ceiling. The more I dwelled on it, the more I realized a ceiling was not just a ceiling. The implications were much deeper and multi-dimensional. It was a heavy moment for me. But Honey was laughing her ass off. Lifting our heads to look over the landscape of our lower bodies, James and I realized Honey was having a moment of her own. She was looking up our towels at our balls. She said, "How do you guys walk around with those things?"

41 … I had a doctor's appointment this morning. He pointed at the MRI and said the fall at Honey's funeral left "a cicatrix" on my brain. This cicatrix may be causing the increase in the number of seizures I'm having. He wrote a new prescription. "Something stronger," he said. "You may experience side effects, an increase in auras. This is normal at first, but if the frequency of the auras doesn't ebb within a week or two, or if the grandeur of the seizures graduates, I want you to call me." I'm not taking any chances. Seizures or no seizures, things are coming too clearly for me now. I threw the prescription in the trash on my way out. It's not the drugs. I know in my heart, the writing, Honey's story, will save me.

42 … I was cleaning the house, doing dishes, sorting mail, folding laundry and putting it away when I found the old compact that I used to carry my acid. The flat red canister with a pig sticker on the lid was in my top drawer, in a sock. I opened it and admired the mirror image inside. There was a time when the canister was always full and the canister never left my pocket. Invariably, I tried every batch of acid I bought, before sharing it with anyone else. It was normal, for me anyway, to buy a ten-lot at a time. That way I always had cash in my pocket and acid to share. There was a point during my junior year in high school that I was taking acid every morning. I would wake up at about 5:30 and open the little red compact. I would look myself in the mirror and make a heavy moment out of it. Invariably, there were options for how my day might go. At first, I went with the tried and true – a half white blotter; an ant; a rainbow. Eventually, I started mixing it up and increasing my doses. I'd eat half of a white blotter and half of a coat of arms, or a quarter of a green blotter, one white blotter and half of a windowpane. One or two tabs was normal, but there were a few times I took three. No trip was ever the same as another. By the time I stepped out of the shower I was feeling good. By the time I got on the bus that would take me to school, I had entered a parallel landscape.

43 ... Tripping at school was fun. Walking the corridors between classes was a hoot. There are a lot of fucked up, fake people in this world. The teachers (who had their own maladies) talked about some far out shit most of the time. One of my teachers took the cake, however. Brother Bilson taught biology. Bilson was a pale fat white man with a girlish face, long eyelashes and short, straight black hair. His lips were thin and his gestures were lumbering and feminine. When he spoke it was monotone. When he made a point he widened his eyes and pursed his lips as if he were stretching his sinuses. He was an interesting person to watch but not the person you'd want to invite to your acid trip. It took Bilson to end the I-think-I'll-take-acid-and-go-to-school period of my life. It was third period Bio. I was peaking. It had been an uncertain climb so far – a bad blotter and a good one. I was just trying to keep it together. Bilson was explaining how "everyone can be broken down into a chemical soup of math equations." Slowly I watched my classmates morph into a broth of numbers and mathematical symbols. I was obligated to shake myself free from the hallucination, only I couldn't slow the momentum. The acid was turning on me. The combination was too strong. I watched in horror as the nerdy girl I kissed freshman year turned into a liquid mess on the floor. No one noticed. No one cared, because Bilson was now telling us about his hobby, a skeleton "assemblage" that he'd been building in his free time "for years." I tried not to listen, but it was difficult. Bilson said he prayed while he cleaned the bones. "You can't imagine the concentration it takes to pin and band a complete bird skeleton. Birds are very fragile creatures," he said. My classmates were mesmerized, dripping on the floor. I needed to get out of there but I was frozen. Bilson pointed in my direction. "Ronald," Bilson said, all eyes and sinuses. Ron sat behind me. He was a big effeminate like Bilson. Ron said, "Brother, my cat died last night. Is that something you might be interested in praying with?" Bilson said they could discuss the specifics after class. And that was just about it for me. I laughed out loud and I tried to control myself but a wad of snot shot from my nose and landed on my desk. The class groaned and winced. I grabbed my backpack and left the snot for someone else to clean up.

44 ... Acid was for Fridays only, from then on. And Honey and I were the only true diehards that would do it weekly, without fail. Everyone else, though invited, had backed away from the stuff as Honey and I grew more and more in love with it. It was summer; Honey's folks were going out on their boat almost every weekend so we would trip at Honey's house. When her folks were home, we'd go to the boat or to Cobbs Hill or School One or the train tracks in the heart of the Can of Worms. James was pushing Honey's buttons a lot those days. The stress was a real bugbear. One of the nights, Honey and I dropped after she and James had broken up again. She didn't say anything until we were a few hours in. At that point, I couldn't leave her. For the next several hours we laid head to head in the grass in her back yard. I was trying to make her laugh. She was listing the ways she was right to be away from him. It was a real bummer for both of us, but what could I do? She was my best friend by then. We were communicating with and without words. I got lost in the maze of her fingerprints and climbed the stalks of hair on her head. I swam the oceans in her eyes and got washed away in her blood. For all she had done to keep their relationship alive ... for all the insults and put downs, the peril she put her body and spirit through ... just to stay with James ... I wondered if it was worth it. I wondered if she cared. She said, "I don't think I care anymore, H." I told her that I understood. It was a changing point for all of us.

45 ... I am a prisoner of my own recovery. The old house is haunted by loose nails and dry boards. Mice scale the crumbling insulation in the walls. I can't sleep. Dad is snoring. I went downstairs to steep and spice some milk. While it warmed, I walked through the rooms. There are scores of photos of the house and of the cemetery in our back yard. The house was once the central funeral office for the Mount Hope Cemetery. In one

of the photos on one of the bookshelves, two men preside over a casket in what is now our living room. When the milk was ready, I went back upstairs and sat down at the typewriter. It's a windy night. There must be leaves in the streets of Iowa City by now, animals storing nuts, students wearing coats instead of shorts and skirts. This is a nice image to start with. I need something more than Honey to focus on.

46 ... This typewriter makes me feel clumsy. With each word, I stumble toward the truth. Each piece of paper loads into the rollers like a body being wrapped in a carpet. The strike of each letter is a gunshot. Sometimes, I never begin. Whose truth is this anyway? I'm filled with doubt, but I have convinced myself to share these intimate horrors. I have convinced myself that everyone has something they will always carry with them. Am I wrong?

47 ... On the weekends, I used to like going to Dad's office. He had a new Apple computer that made it easy to work on my school papers. I was working on something for school, I don't remember what, when the office telephone rang. It was Dad. He said, "Come home." I asked him what was up. He said, "I need you to come home now." When I arrived at the house, there was a strange car parked out front, a strange man in the living room, and my stash was on the counter in the kitchen. There were Tupperware containers with baggies of marijuana, the digital scale, my kif kit, glass bong, my brass pipe, rolling papers and blunts, bottles of pills, and a leftover box of glow sticks from a rave I'd been to. Thankfully, he hadn't found the compact with the acid. Dad introduced me to Officer *Friendly* and asked me to sit down on the couch across from them. Officer *Friendly*

then told me a story. He said, "A very long time ago, my car ran out of gas, in front of your house. I was on my way to the store to buy diapers for my infant. The lights were on, so I knocked on the door and asked if I could use the telephone to call for some help. Your father let me use the telephone and he offered to take me up the street to get some gas. And, because the store was next to the gas station, we went to the Wegman's supermarket so I could pick up the diapers I needed. Your father and I were both living like a dime cost a quarter those days, but he bought the diapers for me ..." Dad interrupted Officer Friendly, saying "As a gift, from one father to another." Officer Friendly nodded in agreement. Dad took the story from there. "Today, Officer *Friendly* knocked on my door again. Only now, he is a police officer. He is part of a team that had been watching you and your friends." Dad was staring into his lap, ashamed. Dad said, "Officer *Friendly* remembered my gesture from twenty years ago and he wanted to return the favor. He wanted to let you know...." Officer *Friendly* nodded and said, "It's not to late to stop doing what you're doing. You can change the direction of your life. All of that, in there, on the counter. That's a dead end. That's nowhere you want to be. But it's also somewhere you are going. You have time, Henry. You still have time to change." It was a heavy concept, considering that I was, in that moment, extremely high and buzzing from the adrenalin. "What do you have to say for yourself?" I started to say something, but I paused before saying, "Two things." They were both eager to hear what I had to say. "First. Can I see your ID?" If Dad were a hitter, I'm sure he would have nailed me. He said, "You're not taking this very seriously, Henry. This is very serious." Officer *Friendly* obliged. He showed me his badge. The name wasn't *Friendly* but the gold shield was sewn into a black leather wallet. It looked legitimate. "And," I said, "What's with the glow sticks?" Dad answered, "You tell us. Is that some kind of new drug you kids are doing?" I didn't have the ground to be sarcastic, but I felt the need to inform them. "Sometimes glow sticks are just glow sticks."

48 ... Dad was more than disappointed. He was angry. He closed the door

behind Officer *Friendly*. I started to say something, but he very succinctly stopped me. "Shhh ... I'm going to tell this story ... When Officer Friendly came to the door this morning, I told him he had the wrong kid ... but he ... he assured me ... in more ways than one ... the police have been listening to our telephone calls, Henry ... they have a tap on our phone! ... *Our telephone*!" He pointed toward the kitchen. "You are going to get all of *that, out, of, this ... our house*! Now." Dad re-gained his composure and said, "How could you get involved in this? How could you be involved with drug dealers and thieves? Do you know that you've been photographed, that the police have a file on you? On you, Henry!" He stuttered. "Tell me ... Do you understand how this man just put his job and his family on the line for us? ... To save your ass?" I had no time for empathy. I was trying to figure out how much they really knew. How many times had I'd been followed, how many conversations had I had that led to something illegal. If they were watching me, they were certainly watching Honey and James. I felt like an idiot for not noticing but I was stoned all the time. "It all makes sense," Dad said. "The glazed look in your eyes ... your staying out till all hours of the night ... your complacency ... what a laughingstock ... boy, you really had me fooled Henry ... I think you need to ask yourself some questions now ... I'm going to lay down for a while ... When I wake up I want everything, and I mean *ev-ree-thing*, out of the house ... and I want you on the couch." He started up the stairs. "Dad," I said. He paused just long enough to say, "Not another word." The only time Dad referred to the incident again was in passing, a few days later. We were making dinner. He paused when he entered the pantry. Without looking at me, he said, "I've lost a lot of good friends to drugs ... these are people I loved, Tip ... I don't want to see that happen to you ... I don't want to go to your funeral. I don't think I could survive that."

49 ... Old habits die hard. I had been high for years. Once word got around that I was burned the scene dried up. Doors didn't open, phone numbers changed. The worst part about it was the sobriety, the slow down, the traffic jam. I hadn't felt that miserable in years. Thankfully, there is an

inertia, a momentum, in being high for so long. No matter how or what direction the rest of the world happens to be moving, you continue to move in stereo.

50 ... Those days, I was writing in a marble composition notebook, spending Tuesday nights at the Java House downtown. They had a weekly poetry series and I was locked in the first night I went down there, at my professor Jaja Paduzzi's suggestion. The night started with a mug of sweet Chocolate-Raspberry coffee. I found a table in the back and sat there for a while, smoking, drinking, drawing, writing. The front of the Java House was all windows. There was a small stage and piano positioned along the front windows. At around seven, a spotlight illuminated the stage and a woman in jeans and a black vest took the stage. She addressed the patrons loitering at the counter, sitting at the tables, and on the sidewalk out front and set a time frame for the evening's reading. Over the next hour or so, several people stood in the spotlight. Some of them read poetry. One guy sang a song and played a guitar. A couple got engaged, and an old guy did magic while reciting Byron. It seemed that no matter what you were into, the Java House was a popular place to be.

51 ... Tuesday nights at The Java House were busy. The Open Mic performances had become quite a draw. I was attending regularly, watching and listening, hanging out. One Tuesday night, the counter girl with the short blond hair came outside and lit a cigarette. She seemed nervous. "Rough night?" I asked. "Let's see," she said, lighting a personal tirade that ended with "you know ... fuck it ... it's just a job, right?" I agreed with her and let her smoke the rest of her cigarette in peace. As she went

inside, she said "Thanks." Moments later, the host enthusiastically introduced the counter girl as "our very own Melinda!" Melinda took the stage wearing her apron. She immediately had our attention. She whispered into the microphone, "This is called Rough Night ... Someone ask me how my night's going." Several people replied. Melinda began. "For starters some of y'all need to bathe more, and brush your teeth. Secondly, some of y'all need to tip more, y'all need to tip more, tip more. And some of y'all need to understand, the espresso machine is busted. It's broken. Broken means it doesn't work. Broken means, you can't have a triple shot mocha-fuckin-chino tonight. You're gonna have to drink drip. We have three different flavors and one type of decaf, and no I don't have my period. No there isn't something up my ass. No, this isn't my first day, it's not even a bad day. I did, however, meet my ex-boyfriends new girlfriend tonight. Nice to see you again Jimmy." She pulled her hand out of her apron pocket with her middle finger extended. A bunch of people looked around for Jimmy. "Let's see..." Melinda continued. "I have chocolate sauce in my hair, chocolate chips in my boot, and a dollar-fifty in my bank account ... there's nowhere in the world that I'd rather be than at the fucking Java House ... It's a good job, right? Some of you fuckers don't even have that! I should feel blessed. I should feel honored! But, you know what ... I don't ... I'm not spoiled. I'm not shallow. I just don't need this shit ... I don't need this shit! ... Fuck you, and fuck you, a very special fuck to you ... and oh, totally, fuck you ... I quit." Melinda stepped off the stage and threw her apron toward the pastry cooler. Then she walked out. Everyone was stunned into silence. Moments later Melinda appeared behind the counter. She was smiling. She looked some poor lady in the eye and said, "What can I get you?" The audience erupted in applause. The host whistled and said, "That's why we love her. Melinda!" It was the first time I realized that poetry didn't have to be so serious. Poetry didn't have to live on the page. Poetry was an extravagance of breath – the flight of a bird, the path of a cloud – not the poem itself, but a freeing of the soul.

52 ... Jaja reserved an auditorium for our class one day. Three Nuyorican Poets were in town on the *Aloud* book release tour. We filed into the audi-

torium and took our seats. Jaja introduced the poets, Tracy Morris, Willie Perdomo, and Mike Tyler. I'd never heard of any of them. Jaja explained a few things about performance poetry and then each poet gave a performance of their work. Tracy read first. The performance was graceful and eloquent, classy and strong. She had a point. I forget what it was. Willie performed after Tracy. He presented a piece in two or three languages with a slow urbanized tempo. He also had a point. I don't remember what it was because Mike took the stage. He started his performance by pushing a desk to the wall. He laid the podium on its side, on top of the desk, and a positioned a cheap folding chair on the podium. He positioned the overhead projector next to the cheap folding chair and turned the projection lamp on. Then Mike climbed the furniture mountain until he was standing on the illuminated overhead projector and the cheap folding chair. He removed a part of the ceiling and poked his head into the open space above the acoustic panels. He was moving his foot around on the projector – which was projecting the image against one of the far walls – while he read (or performed) a piece that no one really heard because everyone was laughing and asking each other *what the fuck* he was doing. Mike got down but he left the furniture where it was, like an illuminated mountain that led to the dark inner workings of the building. We all applauded and Jaja thanked the poets, adding, "We have the auditorium for another hour. Does anyone want to read?" No one wanted to go on after Mike. He had taken over the room. Jaja pointed at me and said, "Henry." I tried to convince Jaja that I didn't have anything with me. "Bullshit," Jaja said. "You're always holding."

53 … I was usually holding. This much was true, but I traded out my old notebook a few days earlier and the only new poem I had was something about watching a girl fall asleep in one of my classes. It was a tender poem, something I read very slowly. When I finished, Mike Tyler shouted from the back of the room, "You need to get laid man!" I was devastated. The rest of my classmates were snickering, Jaja was smiling. I sat down and a few other students read their work. As each person finished, com-

ments were made but we didn't hear another peep from Mike. I was so upset that I started seeing auras in the long auditorium curtains. I snuck out. I needed air. I found a spot out on the quad and waited it out. That night, Jaja, Tracy, Mike and Willie walked into the Java House as I was signing up for the Open Mic. The poets were staying at Jaja's house. He was entertaining them. Considering that the Java House hosted the only weekly poetry reading in town, it was inevitable, perhaps, that they would spend the evening there. "Oh, good," Jaja said. "I'm glad to see that you're reading tonight. Show-them-the-business-end of it." Jaja invited me to join him and the Nuyoricans at a table in the back of the main room. I joined them, but I was pre-occupied, thinking of ways to get my name off the list. Tracy could tell I was nervous. She said, "Don't worry about what happened today. Michael is a puppy dog. Heckling is his way of encouraging you." Mike was listening. He said, "No it isn't. You stepped onto my stage. I *had to* piss on you." Tracy asked me when I was scheduled to go on. "It's random," I said. "Anytime."

54 ... I was talking to Melinda, the short blond counter girl, when my name was called. I was debating what to read. "You should improv," Melinda said. "Fuck breaking a leg, you should break your face. Free your mind." I didn't think I was ready. Poetry was still very much a part of the page, a trapping of time, buried alive somewhere in the middle of a note-book cemetery, among other notebook cemeteries. I imagined what that must feel like, to be a word trapped in a poem in a notebook in someone's pile of notebooks. Mike may have pissed on me that afternoon, but I was going to impress Melinda now. I took the stage and I looked at my note-book, at the pages, and the bodies of letters and words I'd created. I said, "I'd like to dedicate this piece to ... the memory of Mike. Because Mike carried his notebook everywhere." I put the notebook down and closed my eyes. I said, "Mike wrote in his notebook every day. Mike loved his notebook. But, what Mike didn't know was that he was kind of a dick. In fact, one night ... when Mike was at home writing in his notebook, two very large men that Mike did not know came to his door and took

him away. Maybe out of instinct or habit, Mike brought his notebook. He started writing things he remembered about the kidnapping. He remembered the license plate number. The words on the patch on one of the guy's shirts. The aromatic profile of the trunk of the car they threw him into. When the car finally stopped, they opened the trunk again and knocked Mike out. When Mike woke up, he was in a wood box. It was dark and hot and silent. He screamed and clawed at the inside of the container, but he never got out. He never got the word out. He was too late to save himself. Too late to contradict the present. As Mike suffocated and died he managed to scribble the last few words he would ever write. This would be his magnum opus; the thing that would define him when the suburbs finally reached out to develop the field where Mike's body was found. There, on a brand new page, scribbled in pencil, were Mike's final words. '*All I ever wanted was to get laid.*'"

55 ... The next morning, I woke to a beam of light coming through Melinda's curtains. From that moment, we were off and running. It was a faster relationship than I was used to. I felt like I was always trying to keep up. Melinda's style was high gear, high speed. She did what she wanted, when she wanted, damn the consequences. Almost every time we saw each other we were trying a new position or technique to reach literary or physical orgasm. Some things worked. Some didn't. Eventually, with Melinda's help, I found comfortable rhythms on stage and in the bedroom. "It's important," Melinda said, "to lead your audience toward a desire." On stage, I enjoyed re-creating experiences from my own life – a found poem scribbled on a napkin on laundry day; the influence of nature; a problem solved. I knew I was onto something when Melinda paused during an impromptu reverse cowgirl and said, "The owners [at the Java House] want you to headline Tuesday night. Come with me?" I was ready if she was.

56 ... I didn't consider the possibilities. I made the flyer as a joke. I saved a few copies in my posterity box and pinned the rest around campus. The background photograph is of a guy riding a bike on a high wire. The flyer reads "COME ALL! HENRY NIGHTEEN! LEVITATIONS & INCANTATIONS! ORAL NUDITY! $5 GETS YOU IN THE DOOR. 7 P.M. TUESDAY, AUGUST 3, JAVA HOUSE, 322 GIBBS STREET. DOWNTOWN. BE EARLY. STAY LATE. LIMITED SEATING." No one was more surprised with the turnout than me. By the time Dad and I walked into the Java House, it was standing room only. Melinda found some counter space for Dad and poured a cup of decaf for him. She touched my arm and said, "Give me a hand. I need to set up another speaker outside." We lifted the heavy black speaker and passed Jaja at the doorway. Jaja shoved a smile into the side of his face and said, "Big turn out. This better be good or the lions you invited to dinner are going to have you for dessert." Melinda and I set up the speaker, she said the take at the door was more than they'd expected. I would get my cut at the end of the night. I didn't tell her I would be leaving for Iowa with it. I was tempted to tell her, but I knew she'd be fine with a casual goodbye. Melinda prepared the stage and turned on the spotlight. The patrons grew loud enough to drown out the bean grinder but not the steamer. I stepped behind the counter for a bottle of water when Honey, Raine, and Lynnae walked in. I hadn't seen any of them since I'd been burned. When I asked Melinda if she could help my friends she said, "You know where everything is. Make it yourself." I took Honey's order first. Her eyes were like water on ice. "Is this all for you?" she asked. "No," I said. "It's for you."

57 ... Melinda took the stage and tested the microphone. I was in the audience, swollen with paranoia. The few pieces I prepared for the reading were new, some had barely seen the light of day. Melinda arrested the frenzy, "Thank you all for coming. Tonight, is kind of a special night.

We've been doing these readings for five years, you've all been coming here for most of that. So thank you. And thank you again because as of tonight we have enough dough to expand the Java House into the next storefront!" The patrons cheered. "We'll be knocking down the wall this weekend, so we will be closed on Saturday and Sunday. But next Tuesday, you will see a more open …" she paused then finished with, "Space for poetry!" Howls came from all corners of the coffee house and outside on the sidewalk. Melinda was reading the introduction I had prepared but then she stopped. She found me in the audience and scoffed at my introduction. "You defy gravity? … Cease your conscious effort to be someone cool and be someone original? … What is this crap?" Melinda went off script. "Tonight, we have a young writer who …" Melinda had a talent for pacing. "Let's say, he's going places." The way she said it was a little on the nose. I found out later that Dad spilled the beans about Iowa. I hadn't told anyone. "Our poet tonight is en route to the Writer's Workshop at the University of Iowa where he will be studying with the best writers the world has to offer." The cat had completely left the bag. Honey found me in the crowd and gave me a look. Melinda continued, "Henry is a regular here, we love him and we'll miss him. Please give a warm Java House welcome … to … Hen-ry! Nigh-teen!"

58 … I was tense and nervous. Melinda had blown me up into an automatic disappointment. I stepped on stage and felt the cold weight of the audience in my cheeks. There was a jellyfish swimming around in my head. It passed by my right eye and I froze. The audience was staring, still talking. The steamer on the espresso machine shrieked. The coffee grinder brought the auditory chaos to a climax as the jellyfish swam across my field of vision. I reached for it and spoke into the microphone, "Shh."

59 ... I was able to keep the seizure at bay, but it affected my performance. There was a ringing in my ears. I was forced to project. My idiosyncrasies were magnified. I was animated. The aura passed during the final piece. It was a poem I dedicated "to HR." It was homage to Allen Ginsberg's *Please Master*. I hadn't planned on reading it, but I was caught in the moment. I was going to miss Honey more than anyone. Then again, I was leaving because of her, because I had sinned to get her. I hadn't planned any of it. The pieces all just kind of fell into place on a random Friday afternoon. Honey and I were high. She was lying on the couch in her living room. I was sitting on the floor next to the couch, seducing her. It wasn't easy, but she gave in. She let me kiss her. "Once. No tongue." The moment our mouths touched, we were unstoppable. That night, we joined Raine and Alise on a weekend road trip to visit some friends who had a house in Binghamton. Before we left, Raine rolled a blunt. We smoked more in the car. By the time we got to Binghamton, I was so high that I was strobing, living eternities between moments. Raine's friends were having a trimming party. Their marijuana harvest was drying in one of the bedrooms and everyone was cutting and bagging leaves. We smoked more dope and ate more ganja cookies that night than a small village has a right to. When everyone crashed, Honey and I were offered a pillow and a sleeping bag at the foot of someone's bed. We talked quietly until I decided to go for it. "What are you doing?" Honey asked. "Unbuttoning your pants," I said. "Okay," Honey replied, undoing mine. It took a lot of work keeping quiet but I was sure, this was going to be a very big problem.

60 ... James came to me with a problem. He needed money for something big. "And quick." I pried, but he wouldn't tell me what was going on. He was panicked, almost frantic with despair. We brainstormed. I wasn't remotely interested in helping James anymore. I was more interested in helping myself to Honey. "I've got it," I said. I told him that Myra was pet sitting for a couple who was in Hawaii. Myra wasn't staying at the house.

She had the pet at her apartment downtown. The house was empty. I told him that we'd been there only the day before, that there was a chest of jewelry in one of the bedrooms. Myra and I hadn't spoken in months, but James knew how rich she was. He asked me why I'd want to rip off my *girlfriend*. He said, "Doesn't sound like you." In the end, I convinced him that I hated to do it, but it would be the easiest way to help him. I asked him one more time what he needed the money for, but James told me not to worry about it. He said, "You handle the logistics and I'll handle the back end. I can cut you in at thirty percent." My response was a handslap. "Bros before hos," I said. "I'll set it up." I took the city bus to Henrietta and walked around until after dark. I needed the perfect house. I found it in a quiet residential neighborhood. There was a security sign on the front lawn and there were enough shadows to hide a potential burglar. The owner, a bear of a man, drove up the street in a truck and parked in the garage. His young blond spouse was athletic. There were no kids, no dogs that might alert the owner to James' entry. I waited until the house went dark to throw the security sign in the bushes. I knew James would look for a low-level window to enter the house, so I went to those windows and used a razor blade to remove the security system warning stickers. The last light to go out was on the second floor. I called James from a pay phone. I gave him the address and said, "The jewelry box is in the upstairs front bedroom." James went over it with me and seemed to feel comfortable with the scenario. He would get in easily, but he might not get out. As back handed as it was, this was my play for Honey.

61 … James managed to get a car for the heist. He picked me up and we drove past the house a few times. He parked up the street and exited the car, disappearing into the shadows around the house. I counted to sixty and quietly got out of the car. The sidewalk was hard and cold. I picked up the pace as I turned the corner. My heart was pounding. My gut was in a knot. Several police cars raced darkly toward the house. It would be difficult, but I could talk my way out of this one with James. I wasn't sure he could do the same with the cops.

62 … The trip to Wegman's with Dad this morning overloaded my senses.
There were too many people, there was too much light, too much food.
I came to my room to take a nap. As I was falling asleep, the telephone
rang. I heard Dad's side of the conversation. "What time?" he said. I woke
up several hours later and went downstairs. I got a soda from the fridge
and sat down on the couch next to Dad. He was watching Highlander. He
muted the Tv and said, "You're having lunch with Jack and Jean tomorrow." I asked what Honey's parents wanted. "Why the arranged lunch?"
Dad said, "Jack didn't want to say. I'll pick you up here at noon, they'll
bring you home when you're done." I asked if we could watch something
else and reached for the remote control. Dad said, "No. I'm watching
this." I leaned back in the couch cushions and opened the can of ginger
ale. I feel like a kid again. If only I was, I could do some things over again.

63 … I took Dramamine to help me sleep tonight. It made me nauseous
instead. I can't lie down. It makes things worse. If I sit up, I'm fine, so
I come back to the table, back to this hard chair, this loud Royal typewriter. Honestly, I feel safe here – facing the door, my back to the corner
– guiding my fingers to press the keys that swing the arm that lands the
type against the ink ribbon. Since Jack's call, my memories are a merry-
go-round of photographs with shuffled captions. How do I articulate this
knot? … Dad just came to the door. My lamp is bright. He squinted and
probably meant to say *stop typing*. What he said was, "It's late. We both
have big days tomorrow. Get some sleep."

RUNNING

64 ... The key to running away is to convince the observer that you're running toward something.

65 ... The morning Dad and I left for Iowa he merged the old white sedan onto the interstate and gunned it. A shudder of energy rolled through the car. There was just one last hill to get over. I could feel the tension. Dad needed the car to make it – to Iowa and back. This hill was the proving ground, the first big challenge. Dad leaned forward and focused on the sounds the engine was making. "Come on," he said. We passed one car, then another, and finally a couple of trucks. We were going to make it. Dad smiled and pulled into the right lane as the transmission shifted into a lower gear. There was an opening in the clouds on the grade horizon. A small moving-truck passed us first, then a queue of tractor-trailers. Everyone we had passed at the bottom of the grade was now passing and pulling away from us. The sedan shuddered and slipped into a lower gear. Dad took the gamble. He pressed the gas pedal to the floor and the struggling sedan took off. We crested the hill and gave each other a high five as the gray-scale city of my youth vanished in the rearview and the plains of my future unfurled around us.

66 ... Jack and Jean made sandwiches and a salad for our lunch today. Honey's absence was a heavy weight. We sat in the breakfast den that overlooked the back yard and the pool. Nothing and everything had changed. We fumbled with small talk until it grew awkward. I was staring. I could see Honey in the both of them. Jean urged Jack to tell me what they needed to tell me. He got straight to the point. Honey had a will. He asked me if I knew about it. I didn't. Jack said, "She revised it recently" but the new will hadn't been notarized. "We're willing to honor Honey's wishes." I found it strange that Honey would have a will at all. Jack said, "Honey left you some things." I asked him what kind of things. He led me to Honey's room and said, "She left you everything 'cool'," and made a gesture. I didn't understand what Jack meant until he opened Honey's bedroom door. There were several round red stickers with white letters that read COOL. There were other COOL stickers on the bookshelf, the shag carpet, the stereo, a necklace from Hawaii, a Life Saver frisbee. "I think she knew that she wasn't coming back," Jack said. "I'll get you a box."

67 ... The smell of a person can stay with a place. Honey's room was saturated with her. I could smell her in the fibers of the curtains, the bedding, and pillows. I have a memory of Honey sitting cross-legged, on the white shag carpet. We were high, or getting there. She stuck one of the COOL stickers on my forehead and said, "You're cool." Now, there was a COOL sticker in her place, on the carpet. Jack returned with a brown cardboard box. "Do you know why she would have left you these particular things?" My lip quivered. I told him, "Memories." Jack said, "There's a lot that won't fit into this box. I'll give you a few minutes." He left me in Honey's room. I set the box down and wiped my face with my hands and sobbed, wondering why she would want me to have these things. I bent down.

"Where the hell am I going to put a white shag carpet?" I didn't want it. I didn't need it. It smelled like Honey's dog, Rufus. I pulled on the COOL sticker. The adhesive held onto the shag and the edge of the carpet lifted. Under the carpet was a COOL sticker stuck to a key beside a knothole in one of the floorboards. There was a keylock in the knothole. Honey was telling me something. I tried the key. The mechanism was quiet. The floorboard came up. It was a secret compartment, the compartment Honey told me about. There was something in the darkness but there was no time to be sure. I heard the stairs creak. I closed the latch, pocketed the key, dropped the carpet, and moved the COOL sticker to a small white bear. I was holding the bear over the brown cardboard box when Jack and Jean came in. "Can we help?" Jean said.

68 ... I was washing the dishes when Dad came home from work. He spoke with someone at the University of Iowa today. They're mailing leave of absence forms. My food plan has been canceled and a bill for outstanding costs will be sent to the house. "You've paid for your dorm room through next May." I asked Dad how it all got handled so effortlessly. He said, "I love you. That's how."

69 ... It's been a month now since Dad and I traded western New York's rolling hills for an undulating Pennsylvania rainstorm. Interstate 80 was laid out like a ribbon toward a sherbet-colored horizon. To think that monstrous highway extended from one end of the country to the other and in all directions from any point along the way was discombobulating. I tried to focus on the landscape, on the small towns that stretched from the highway to the skyline. It was all just too massive. I had never been west of

Toledo. The world was opening up and to be honest, I was a little scared. Dad and I had been together for years and now, I realized that the fork in the road was coming, that this time together would come to an end. Dad picked up on the heaviness. He said, "We'll get there, Tip. We'll make it. Together, we can do anything."

70 ... The house where Dad grew up is in Brecksville. He turned the old white sedan down the steep driveway into the woods and over the creek. The single-level house was built from old river stone and granite. Dad's father, my grandfather, was a stone mason. Grandma came out to greet us. She has taken to wearing luxury sweat suits these days. She said, "My two travelers! You both look so tense! Come inside, bring your things, we'll have you loosened up in no time." When my grandfather died – after fifty-two years of marriage and raising four children who matured into complex, successful, domesticated adults – Grandma was left in the family home alone. It was difficult for her at first, but over time, she settled into a regular schedule with the members of the family who lived in town. Dad and his brother had moved away long ago. Now, I was doing the same. It made this visit a special occasion for all of us.

71 ... Before long, we'd eaten twice, with and without visitors. First, Maddie, Marsha and Max came by. Maddie is Dad's younger sister. Max is her husband. Marsha is their daughter. They were on their way to Sandusky for the weekend. They moor their boat outside a theme park every summer. I spent a few weeks there one year. It was a good time. Marsha is one of the coolest girls I know. We were both kind of wild and untamed that year. I'd just gotten my drivers license and she had a lot of cute friends

who liked to get drunk. Maddie and Max just kicked back and relaxed most of the time. They work hard during the week, he as a construction foreman and she as a travel agent. They wanted to wish Dad and I luck on the trip. They only stayed a few minutes, leaving as Leslie and Robert pulled into the driveway. Leslie is Dad's oldest sister. She reminds me a lot of Prudence. She's short, thin, and high energy. Robert's my cousin. He's fifteen years younger than I am. Thomas – Leslie's husband and Robert's father – was working. He sent his regards via a noogie for Dad and a kick in the shin for me. Robert carried out each greeting proudly. Leslie apologized for Thomas and for Robert and we sat at the table while Grandma finished preparing dessert. Dad asked how things were. "Things are good. They're great," Leslie said. "A little stressful maybe, we're being investigated. There's no substance to it, but ... Robert, sweetie, why don't you and Henry go play in the other room." Grandma commented from the kitchen. "There are toys in the rec-room!" Everyone still sees me as a kid. I get it. I guess what they don't know can't hurt them.

72 ... I wanted to sleep-in this morning but Dad knocked on my door and said, "I'm making breakfast." I begrudgingly told him I'd come down. In the kitchen, Dad was making scrambled eggs with bacon and tomatoes. I asked him what *the occasion* was. He said, "The mail came. You got a postcard." When I got downstairs, I looked through the daily mail. The postcard was a photograph of a laughing carnie. I turned the card over. There was no message, just the letter, *M*. "Who's it from?" Dad asked. I looked at the front and back of the card again. "I don't know," I said. But I knew. It was James. He was sending me a signal. But what was the M for? *Murder*? Maybe.

73 … It was dark when we left Grandma's house for Iowa. The morning was a wash of small towns and outlands until we came to a standstill in Gary, Indiana. The sedan was overheating. Dad turned off the air and turned on the heat. I rolled down the window. There were enough cars and trucks and buses to sigh. "Well," Dad said. "We *were* an hour ahead of schedule." Up ahead, there was a road crew on the side of the highway. They weren't working. They were only talking. I gave one of the guys the finger as we gained momentum. It pissed him off. He yelled after the car, but we were going again.

74 … The tight spaces between cars and trucks grew to distances. Dad and I weren't the fast ones. We weren't the slow ones. The cars in front of us, the trucks behind us, everyone advancing a culture I'm sure only some of us believed in. It was a complex mirage of colorful tones and spaces. There was a tempo, a duration. If I were a skilled listener, I might have understood what the highway was telling me. Iowa. "Iowa." I whispered the word to myself until it lost all definition. What the fuck was I doing? *Where* was I going? The countryside was flat and gold, one depressing farm after another. By the looks of it, Honey was right. *Iowa was nowhere.* I imagined that Dad would come to a similar insight, and somewhere along the way he would come to an exhilarating stop at the far end of a cornfield, kick me out into the dust and speed off. We were driving into purgatory. Our entire civilization was devolving into branded oases where our citizens converged to polish and replenish our imperfect machines. It was terrifying, mesmerizing. America the beautiful was America the hideous. There was no turning back. This was going to get ugly.

75 … I'll never forget the first time I saw the Mississippi River. The sedan topped an extended grade. The long wide watercourse spread out before us. Its size created enough of a climactic effect to clear the clouds we'd been driving under for hours. In the river, freighters and smaller boats stitched white lines. In that moment, I found myself without much of an emotional net and a chest full of floundering sensitivities. Maybe that's always been my curse. I am too soft. Like everything else in my life, when it came to the big things I ran away. I tried to forget. Moments after we crossed the bridge and rose up out of the river valley, Dad pointed at a sign. "Iowa – You make me smile." Dad patted the dashboard and flashed the headlights and honked the horn. We weren't in Iowa City yet, but Dad and I gave each other a high-five as another car passed us on the right. The driver was a girl my age. She was cute. She had seen the hubbub, probably noticed the New York license plate. She smiled and accelerated into this memory. It felt good to breathe a little, to realize that there might be other options in life. To understand that there could be other women in my future. I hooted. Dad hollered. I felt alive. Vibrant. Free.

76 … The line to dormitory row began on Highway 80. The off ramp onto First Avenue was lined with luggage-laden vehicles in various forms of caravan. Dad eyed one of the new economy hotels just off the highway. There was a sign at the corner of the parking lot and another under the lobby awning, in the shade – "Welcome back students!" Dad checked in. I watched the line of vehicles creep toward the university. Dad came out with a couple of cold sodas and a room key. "Do you want to drop anything off before we head to the dorm?" I wanted to get there. I wanted to see it, to put a name on it. "Okay," Dad said. "Let's do this!" He got us back in line and kept an even pace, rarely stopping completely. He preferred coasting to pausing. The sedan was struggling with the heat though. Dad had to turn the heater on to keep the gauge at the lower end of the red line. We turned left onto Riverside, selecting a few restaurants where we might eat later. The queue continued moving slowly toward a hillside spot-

ted with buildings closely packed together and surrounded by trees. Signs and police were diverting cars at Grand Avenue and Burlington Street. We inched forward, toward THE DORMS, up Burlington, onto Clinton Street where I began a mental list of the places where I'd try my new ID. One of the places was called *The Airliner*. I could remember that.

77 ... Dormitory row was across the street from fraternity row. The dorms were large apartment buildings. The fraternities were old brick party houses decorated with Greek letters, inflatable pools, picnic benches, cars, tiki huts, and miscellany. Traffic guards in orange vests used whistles to guide the convoy. Dad asked one of the guards for directions to "Stanley Hall." My request for a single dorm room hadn't been filled. According to the letter from the residential housing office, the university had too many incoming students and a lack of places to put them. I would have to stay in "temporary housing" until they found somewhere to put me. A volunteer pointed to an open parking space, told us where to register. The line was decorated with doe-eyed freshman and their parents, pushcarts stacked with boxes and hanging clothes, futon frames, mountain bikes and exercise balls, skis and snowboards, Tvs, couches, refrigerators, rolls of carpet, stuffed animals, a wind vane, street signs and big clocks, a barber pole, a life size statue of Elvis Presley, suitcases, a moose head, a drum kit, guitars, a partial mannequin, mirrors, cookware, computers, a globe, a doll house, a surfboard, plants, stereos, fans, lamps, skateboards, tools, toys, a suit of armor, a stuffed bird, a palm tree, ice skates, a pedestal, slats of wood, a stuffed penguin, and a section of a white picket fence. "We're not waiting. There," Dad said, pointing to a weakness in the university's planning. There was a door that was not being watched. Dad led the way. As we entered the broad, brick building, Dad pointed to a thermometer in the shade. "One o'nine," he said. "I hope you have air conditioning."

78 … The lady at the Stanley Hall registration desk was overwhelmed. She wrapped her hair in a bun and pinned it. A small fan oscillated beside her. A poster promoting the NEW RULES for Stanley Hall itemized the "DOS AND DON'TS" of student housing. "One person at a time," she said. The parents were starting to lose it. They didn't like the answers or the service they were getting. They were being very vocal about it. Dad rolled his eyes and wandered off while I cut in line. Just behind where we were standing was a lounge. There were several couches and study tables, floor-to-ceiling windows. Dad walked into the lounge and stopped at the piano. I gave the lady behind the counter my information and a copy of the letter from the residential housing office. She assembled a plastic bag with the University of Iowa logo and handed me a key. "You're in lounge three." She held up three fingers and looked me in the eye and pointed. "Go to the end of this hall here. This key works the lounge lock and the front door. If you have questions, there is a folder in your bag with all the information you need. Welcome to Iowa."

79 … The Lounge door was decorated with colorful construction paper balloons. Each balloon had a name on it. Mine was taped to the door near the knob. Dad stepped in first. He spun back into the hall. "Something smells," he wretched. I hadn't taken a breath yet. The lounge was ungodly hot, a wall of windows faced south. Something was rotten or dead or both. I was sweating through my shirt by the time I got the windows open. Dad propped the door. We were able to get some air circulating, but whatever smelled had to go. The lounge looked and felt like a barracks with carpeting. There were five bunk beds lined against one wall, while the opposite wall of windows overlooked the river. At one end of the room was a kitchenette. The kitchenette had a table and a counter, a sink, and one cupboard. There was a telephone, stacked on a telephone book. "Gross," Dad said. He was holding a carton of milk. "Looks like someone left you a welcome

gift." Dad took the carton to the bathroom down the hall. The lounge was clean for the most part. There were two dressers, one desk, and several wood chairs. The bed farthest from the kitchenette was the only bunk that had any shade. I sat down on the mattress as Dad came back into the lounge. "Good, I was going to suggest you take that one," he said. "It's the only one with shade. You might even want to throw your stuff on top," he added. "There are ten beds and only nine balloons. Why don't we unload. Then we'll go celebrate."

80 ... We made two trips using a roll cart to move the heavy things from the car, through the basement, up the elevator, down the hall and into the lounge. Half stunned by the heat and the weight of my storage trunk, Dad asked where I put *the machine*. The machine was a new Apple Powerbook 150 Dad bought for me. He wanted to be sure I took good care of it. I pointed to the lock I had on my storage trunk. It was where I had all of my important shit: the PowerBook, my notebooks, an ounce and half of Mexican brick weed, and the new collapsible bong Raine gave me as a going away present. We pushed the trunk into the corner. Dad knocked on the side of the trunk and said, "You guys okay in there? You packed all your friends in there, right?" I told him it was my notebooks and *the typewriter*. "It's not a *typewriter*, Tip. It's a *computer*," he said. "Top of the line."

81 ... Dad vouched for me when we went out. He said it was the least he could do, that no man should drink alone, and since he was having a beer, I should have one too. There was an enormous tomato on a sign in the parking lot. We drank our first beers, watching the traffic. Our glasses barely had time to get sweaty. The waitress, Heather, brought us another

round and asked if she could take our orders. "Whatever you want," Dad said. "We're celebrating." I ordered potato skins with extra bacon and a BLT. Dad ordered a Bacon cheeseburger. Heather said, "That's a lot of bacon." Dad said, "Perfect. And two more beers, please."

82 … After lunch, Dad wanted to go back to the hotel to relax. There was a pool, he said. We could cool off. He was buzzed. He wanted a nap. As Dad opened the door to the room, we realized there would be privacy issues. He asked if I would take a *leisurely* walk to get ice. "Go check out the pool. Get us a few sodas. I think I saw a game room, here's five dollars. I have to use the bathroom." I took the ice bucket to the vending area and filled it with ice. The polished metal panel on the front of the ice machine was scored with names and graffiti. One of engravings read, *James was here.* I said, "I doubt that."

83 … I put the sodas into the ice bucket and skipped the game room. The pool was calling me. I went out onto the patio and sat down in one of the lounge chairs and fell asleep next to the pool steps. I had a dream that I walked out onto the pool patio. I could see myself laid out in the lounge chair, holding a bucket of ice water in my arms. I reached out to wake myself, to tell myself to get out of the sun, but I startled me. I could see myself standing above me and laid out in the lounge chair, one bucket of ice, one bucket of ice water. I was confused, caught in a loop. Someone leapt into the pool and it woke me. The ice hadn't melted. The sodas were cold. Only a sliver of time had passed. I went back to the room. Dad was in the shower, talking to himself. The circulated air in the room was cool. I covered the ice bucket and turned the Tv on. Dad came out of the bath-

room in a towel with a cloud of steam. I was looking forward to a time when we wouldn't have to share a bathroom. He gave me a look. I said, "What?" Dad meditated on his answer. He said, "You are one of my every-things. I'm going to miss you."

84 … The challenges, the successes, the missed opportunities, the hidden truths had all come to this. Dad turned into the alley between Currier/Stanley and Burge Halls. There was an open parking space on the right. He parked the sedan and turned off the engine. I was ready. He was ready. We got out. I stepped onto the sidewalk. Dad loitered near the front fender. "Do you want to come in?" I said. "I don't think so," he said. "You'll be alright, huh? It seems like a nice town. You've got your room and board. You've got a plan." I looked around. "We'll see, I guess." Dad handed me an envelope. "It's not much, but I think it'll help. Open it later." I put the envelope in my back pocket and tried to absorb the moment. The sun was shining. The heat was building. The trees were lush, green and brown. "Well," Dad said. "I don't suppose it gets more allegorical than this." I think we were both expecting something more dramatic. This parting was too peaceful and serene. But that's when it happened. The moment clicked. Dad's chin quivered. "I love you, Tip. I'm really proud of you." Dad hugged me like it was the last time he would ever see me. "Take care of yourself. You call me if you need anything. Get into the health center as soon as you can. Make sure you're taking your medicine." I told him I would do all of those things. We separated. I said, "I'm sorry, for all the trouble. I never meant for … any of it." Dad took a few steps toward the driver's side and paused with his hand on the handle. "Thank you," he said. "I know." He got into the sedan and started the engine. Rolling down the window, he shifted the great white Lincoln into gear and smiled. "I love you, Henry. Do your best." As he turned the corner onto Clinton Street, Dad tapped out a series of five honks. I waved and replied. "Two bits."

85 … The lounge was locked. I used my key. A tall kid with dark hair met me at the door. He had a broad chin and a boxy frame. He had a joint behind his back. The sweet aroma was unmistakable. "Something smells good," I said. He shut the door behind me and locked it. He extended his hand and said, "I'm Cole." He seemed like a happy kid. He offered me the joint. "The next one," I said. Cole shrugged. "Suit your self. Is anyone with you?" I told him Dad left, that he was going back to New York. Cole said, "*Wow.* I thought it was hard coming in from Cedar Rapids. What the hell are *you* doing in *Iowa*?" I gave him the ten-second summary as he got the joint started again. He walked over to an open window. The more Cole stoked the joint, the more the sweet scent got the better of me. It smelled like some exceptional grass. "You know what Cole, can I get a hit of that?" Cole held out the joint and said, "My friends call me Rugby. And that, my friend, is some *bold* Johnson County indoor." I asked him where Johnson County was. Rugby gave me this big cheeky smile. He said, "You're in it motherfucker! *That shit* was grown up the street!"

86 … That first night in the dorms is kind of a blur. Rugby and I smoked a few more joints in the lounge and went to the store to try my fake ID. It worked. Rugby put the plastic bag of beer into the backpack he brought with him. We were on our way back to the dorm. Rugby was laying the facts of his life on me. His father worked in a factory and his parents had split. He had a fraternal twin brother. "He's a sick kid, always has been. Cardiomyopathy." Rugby said he was going to come out of the University of Iowa with a biochemical engineering major and a cure for his brother's heart problem. "What's your dealio?" Rugby asked. "I've never met anyone from New York. Are you all this way?" I supposed so. I told him about my interest in the Writers Workshop. "I could see that. A writer.

That's a pretty bold move if it works out for you." I hadn't considered that it wouldn't work out. I hadn't considered an alternate future. We turned onto fraternity row. Rugby sighed. He said, "Just think, a few days ago, we were back home with all the people who know us and all the shitty little shit we've done in our lives. Our worlds just changed, my friend. Look at this place! It's a huge fucking playground! We both just got handed a second chance."

87 … Rugby's little speech stayed with me. He made a convincing case. I could reinvent myself. I could be anyone I wanted to be. I drifted among the myriad possibilities as Rugby and I went beer for beer and tequila shot for tequila shot with the newest member of temporary housing. *Justin* was wearing an Iowa Hawkeye jersey. He rubbed his shaved head with the bottle of tequila and named his home town in Southern Illinois. He had been tapped to play for the University of Iowa football team. Justin said, "I'm a runner. I'm fast, and *not* just with a football, if you know what I mean." According to Justin, he was also a bit of a ladies man. Rugby told him he was full of shit. "You don't believe me?" Justin asked. "You're as pretty as my sphincter!" Rugby added. Justin showed us seven "of the ten" hickies different girls allegedly gave him at his going away party. He said "I'd show you the others but then you'd be thinking of my Johnson all the time. You wouldn't be able to think of anything else for the rest of your lives!" Rugby doubted Justin's hickies were hickies at all. He said, "You pinched yourself." But Justin defended his claim by naming several girls names. He remained confident until he got sleepy. We were all getting there, I think, Justin maybe a little faster than the rest of us. He had passed out sitting up. He was snoring. Rugby was laughing as he tipped Justin's chair. Justin woke up falling and accessed the momentum. It's what carried him to bed as Rugby raised a final toast, "To hickies!"

88 … It's not going to be easy to get into Honey's room again. I went to the Riders' house this afternoon with the box they lent me. Jean answered the door. She thought it was *a little weird* that I didn't just throw it out. She became defensive when I asked if I could *get the rest of it*. I didn't mention the secret compartment under the shag carpet or the key in my pocket. All I could manage was "I miss her." Jean stood in the doorway. She wasn't letting me in. She said, "I know you're in mourning, Henry. We all are. Please don't take this the wrong way. Go home. I'll tell Jack you stopped by."

89 … Jack Rider called. Then he came over. I was in my room, pacing around the typewriter, trying to remember what happened next, when Jack arrived. Dad answered the door. He called me downstairs. The three of us sat in the living room while I looked through the box of COOL things Jack brought with him. There was an old bowl from one of the pantry cabinets. It was the bowl I preferred to eat from whenever I was at their house. "Oddly enough," Jack said. "Honey put a COOL sticker on one of my vintage Playboys. It's in the bottom. I didn't know she knew I had those." Honey knew, like most kids know things about their parents. "I wasn't sure if you wanted the shag carpet in Honey's room or not. I noticed there was a sticker on it before you came over last time, then the sticker was gone?" I claimed my amnesia, but I had not forgotten. I moved the sticker to a stuffed animal. The key to the secret compartment was under the type-writer upstairs. Jack knew about the floorboard compartment but he went along with my charade until it became evident that he was there to talk about something specific. Dad asked if we wanted privacy. I don't want Dad to think I'm hiding anything. I invited him to stay. "Fine by me," Jack said. "It's just one thing, Henry. Jean is pretty fragile right now. You know how small things can be very stressful for her. It would mean a lot to me if you didn't just stop by."

90 ... I waited until Dad went to bed before cutting into *The Book of Knowledge*. The hard cover and spine are sturdy. The pages are all heavy stock. It was the perfect choice, the perfect hiding place, a book I never read. The pages glued together nicely. Then, one page at a time I carved out the core, reading about the world, from Charles to Saint Croix. Among the personal effects with COOL stickers that Jack brought to the house that afternoon was Honey's copper and pearl rosary. I strung the rosary through the head of the key to Honey's secret compartment and placed the key inside the hole in *The Book of Knowledge*. I put the book back on my shelf and went downstairs for something to eat. The key is safe for now. Maybe I am too.

91 ... I woke up in the lounge and rolled over in my bunk bed. My bladder was dangerously full. I was still quite inebriated from the tequila and beer. My mouth was dry and webby. I stumbled out of the lounge, using the wall to guide me toward the bathroom. I was half blind, half asleep, half human. By the time I gathered my senses I was fending off an assault. "Oh my God!" someone repeated. It was two very astonished girls. "Who are you? Get out of our room!" They had found things to hit me with. They were swatting me toward the door. It was a rush of pain and pleasure, satisfaction and disbelief. On the one hand, I really needed to piss. On the other, I probably should have been paying more attention. I went back to the lounge and my bunk and to sleep wondering if I had really just pissed in someone's dorm room sink. I said, "Who cares? Assholes probably deserved it."

92 ... The Residential Advisor was not pleased. She was old, a husky blond with an interest in punishing me. The RA asked me if I had anything else to add to my version of the story. I told the RA that I would apologize again if it would make a difference. The RA looked down at a file folder. It wasn't my first folder. She said, "So, a bright young kid from New York comes to Iowa. Why? What's your story?" I gave her a few of the high points, finishing with "I came for the Writer's Workshop." She harrumphed and said, "Tell me something." I agreed, "Whatever you want to hear." She looked me square in the eye and said, "Tell me this will never happen again."

93 ... It hurts to think this much sometimes.

94 ... I've never been good with hunger. When I need to eat I need to eat. I wasn't thinking straight. I hadn't been in Iowa for twenty-four hours and the dormitory authority had already given me a warning. I chastised myself as I walked the long hall across the wide building. I put my frustrated hands in my back pockets and felt the envelope Dad gave me. The cafeteria signs led to a hallway with a bay of windows. An acre of chairs and tables and buffet counters were at the ready, but the lights were off. There was a sign on the door. Board would begin the following Monday.

I opened the envelope Dad gave me, hoping there was a little cash inside. It was a white card with a photograph of a four-leaf clover. There was a phone card inside, and a $50 bill. It could be enough for a short amount of time, if I kept it trim. Under the phone card and the cash was a note. *Do your best. I love you.* "Daddy?"

95 ... I went back to the lounge. Justin and Rugby were still sleeping. It was hot, ten o'clock in the morning. I took a bong hit. A few minutes later I was feeling better. By then, I was re-reading the dial on the thermostat outside. It was already 104°F. Behind the dorms is a pedestrian path that parallels Clinton Street. The path was shaded by trees and punctuated with benches, bicycles, and over achievers getting a head start on the day. The university is prettier than I'd imagined. I walked around the broad white stone Old Capital buildings admiring the enormous columns and framed windows. If there's one thing Dad instilled in me it's an appreciation for things that withstand the touch of time. Turning up Iowa Avenue, I passed a bar, a camera store, a sandwich shop, a pizza place, a pool hall, a bank, and a Mexican restaurant. I wasn't in the mood for any of that. I wanted to wrap my hands around a cold cup of sweet coffee. I was surprised to see how many people were out, dangling bags and gestures, guiding children and dogs. It was all very serene and pedestrian, but then I overheard a woman tell a young girl, "That skirt makes you look like a slut." The girl said, "That's funny. I got it out of *your* closet." I laughed out loud. The woman gave me a look and said, "I wear it better."

96 ... I passed two girls on the street. They were carrying coffee cups. The logo on their cups was one I came to know well in Rochester: a baker

sitting on the lower inside diameter of a bagel. I asked the girls where The Bagel Shop was and followed their directions back to Iowa Avenue. I worked at a Bagel Shop up the street from Dad's place, briefly, about six months ago. I was a quick study. I learned how to make sandwiches and bake bagels and brew a fresh pot of coffee every twenty minutes. They were paying a pittance, but it was legitimate, something I could put on the books. The Bagel Shop in Iowa City looked similar to the one in Rochester. It was a rehabilitated warehouse with muffin-colored hardwood floors, framed monochromatic photographs on off-white walls and powder blue trim. Advertisements featuring short fat animated bakers and giant bagels hung in the windows. It was cool inside, but hectic. I stood in line. Someone brought out a basket of fresh bagels and the customers in line crooned. I could see the baker through the kitchen door. He was working at the big oven with a long wood spatula. The cashier winced when I told her my order – an "oat nut bagel with blueberry cream cheese, sprouts, lettuce and spicy mustard, and an iced hazelnut coffee." When I worked at the Bagel Shop in Rochester, I ate for free. That morning, it cost seven bucks. Dad's $50 would run out quickly. I went to a table under a photograph of a train depot. I was famished. My sandwich was gone before I realized I was eating it. I wanted more, for now and later. I located the day-old-bagel basket on the counter, but I was distracted. The basket was flanked with a sign. "Apply Here."

97 … I asked for and filled out the Bagel Shop application, noting all of my best traits: responsible, reliable, experienced, quick learner, flexible, hard working, and imaginative. I handed the cashier my application and paid for a bag of day-old bagels before going back to my table. She passed the application to the manager who had until then been supervising the assembly of sandwiches. A line stretched from the counter to the front door, but the manager came to the table to meet with me. "Henry!" His name was Tom. Tom sat down and read my application. He said, "You're new in town." I told him I'd gotten in the day before. He was impressed. "You've got initiative." What I had was a limited source of income. "And

you worked at a Bagel Shop in …Rochester?" I told Tom, "It was a great job." I was full of it. I hated every minute of that job. "I can't imagine it would be much different here." He looked down at the application. "How many hours are you looking for?" I told him I hadn't gotten my class schedule yet, but that I would "work around it. Maybe 30 hours a week?" His little universe lit up like it was the Fourth of July the year of the Big Bang. He asked if I could wait. Several minutes later, Tom returned with a red Bagel Bakery shirt and a grin. He said, "I called Rochester. Marjorie said you'd make a good addition to the Iowa team. I can start you off at $6.50 an hour. Marjorie said you're worth it." I didn't remember Marjorie. I didn't know how she could remember me. Tom handed me the shirt. I was befuddled, still drunk, and definitely high. He said, "The job is yours if you want it."

98 … I walked out of the Bagel Shop with a job and a headache. I needed a nap, but when I got back to the lounge there were several strangers and their family members unpacking personal effects. These were the guys I would spend the next few days with, the rest of the balloons I hoped would not show up. A skinny kid with an afro was flanked by his parents who called him *Bird*. The tall guy beside them had long bleached-blond hair and a dead tooth. His name was *Andy*. A woman called *Andy* from the kitchenette and added, "These groceries aren't going to unpack themselves." Andy went to the kitchenette and a black-skinned kid with a bright smile introduced himself as *Shaq*. *Frank*, a chunky Greek kid, was alone, quietly unpacking towels and bedding. *Shane*, was a squat hyper bristle-haired kid. He took a basketball from *Joshua*, a hairy-shouldered fellow in a tank top, and started dribbling around the room. I'm not much for crowds, the doctors say it's the hypervigilance disorder. I said it was *nice* to meet everyone, but then I snuck over to my bunk and laid down. It was *nice* to get off of my feet. The lounge was a buzz of uncertainty. In that moment, I would have wagered that this was the beginning of something new, another life, another time, for all of us. But that's not the way time is arranged. Time is not sequential. Time overlaps time like water coincides

with water. There is no way to sort things out. The separations only mean more connections.

99 ... I spent a few days getting lost around campus, learning what not to eat at the cafeteria, and which vending machines were *groovable*. Grooving was something James started doing in high school. You attach clear packaging tape to the edge of a new one-dollar bill. The dollar bill plus the tape is a *groover*. You use the groover like a dollar bill, only once the vending machine credits you a dollar, you slide the groover back out. These days, most vending machines have security precautions and aren't so easily deceivable. I won't kid you, there is an art to grooving, and a lot of vending companies have picked up on the craft of stealing from vending machines. It took me a while, but once I got the hang of it, I never went anywhere without it. My groover has gotten me out of some tight spots. Most machines will credit you up to two-dollars, some will go as high as three. If you can get access to a change machine, you can make a decent days wage in a few short minutes. Not every vending machine is groovable, however, and from what I'd seen there were security cameras everywhere. That being said, I did find a few older machines scattered around campus where my groover worked great. In a few days I had amassed a backpack full of muffins and candy bars, energy drinks and sodas and a jar full of quarters. When the guys in the lounge asked about my sweet tooth and the quarters, I said, "I found a card game downtown, at the Ped Mall. We play Gin. We play with quarters and Little Debbies." I held up a package of *Cosmic Brownies*, but I never showed any of them my groover.

100 ... There was a line outside the Registrar's Office at Calvin Hall. The queue moved toward a stairwell inside the brick building. These were the last few moments to turn back. Once I declared my major I was stuck with it for two years. You want to see chaos? Tell some poor kid who has no concept of 'the rest of his life' that he has to decide what to do with it *now*. Nine times out of ten, he'll follow the path of someone he trusted or idolized. No one had to tell me what classes to choose. I knew what I wanted. I was going to write my life away. Until the hand of darkness wrapped its fingers over my shoulder to guide me in another direction, I was going to seek out adventure and bleed on the page. I had no interest in medicine or politics. My calling was to harness the breath ... to be full of it ... to seduce you for an invitation to dinner and then insult your cooking. My schedule was filled with classes that *sounded* interesting: History of Relationships, the Art of Rhetoric, and Relaxation Techniques. These classes plus the Writers Workshop was enough to be considered a full-time student. Once I was registered my loans would clear. Someone told me I would have to pay it all back, some day, but for now all I heard was "thousands of dollars" and "your bank account." The line moved slowly and steadily into Calvin Hall through two offices, into a back room where an assembly line of assistants collected our forms, printed our schedules, and laminated our ID cards. In a few short minutes, the federal government deposited thousands of dollars into my account, and I had a schedule I would not be able to keep.

101 ... I waited for Dad to leave for work before going to Raine's this morning. It was nice getting back into the swing of things, hanging with an old friend. We were in Raine's back yard, smoking a joint, when I popped the question. "I need a favor. Whenever the Riders leave the house ... Especially if you think they're going somewhere for a while ... I need you to call me ... I need to get into Honey's room ... If I get what I need, it's worth two-hundred bucks." Raine was suspicious, but agreeable. He said, "I'd help you for nothing. But two c-notes are two c-notes." I had a direct view of the Riders' house, over Raine's right shoulder, through

the neighbor's yard and across the street. Jack and Jean were in the living room. I wasn't wearing my glasses, but I could have sworn he was looking back at me.

102 … The English building, or EPB, overlooked the river and West Iowa Avenue. The Writers Workshop was on the fourth floor. The signage led me to a fluorescent-lit hallway. A large corkboard was littered with announcements: poetry contests, short story anthologies, scheduled appearances, and editorial services. I was excited to be there, to have been accepted under the wing of such a giant literary peacock. Down the hall was a small office. Inside, a woman with long blond hair was surrounded by filing cabinets and folders, and stacks of paper. She said "Hello," and smiled. I introduced myself and said I was there to do whatever I had to do for the Workshop. I showed her my acceptance letter from the University. "Great," she said. "Do you have your manuscript?" I told her I submitted it with my application to the university. "Right," she said. "That was the entry submission. You have to submit another ten pages. Here," she pointed to the last line in a long paragraph. I hate long paragraphs. I barely ever get to the end of them. "Please bring your official submission to the Writers Workshop, Fourth floor of the EPB, by 5 p.m. Friday, August 25 to be considered for the fall semester's workshops." I was moving in reverse. I thought I was in. She saw how distraught and confused I was. "I tell you what, Henry. Why don't you put your manuscript together over the weekend? Slip it under my door by the time the office opens on Monday and…." she pointed at an enormous stack of manuscripts. "I'll include it with the others."

103 … James' disappearance has everyone in a state. I think the only people who really want to find him are the police. Officer Friendly came to the house again today. I almost panicked when I opened the front door, but it was the same old shtick. "No, I haven't heard from James … I will tell you if I do … I know my ass is on the line" … especially if they find him and he talks. But, I honestly don't know where he is. The last time I saw James, he was falling toward the water at the High Point. I was too scared to watch the splash. I don't remember even hearing it. I look at the postcard of the laughing carnie that came from *M*. I know it's from James, but I can't prove it. The zip code on the post mark is from New York City. It would make sense to go there. If there's anywhere to disappear completely, it's New York … One thing's for sure, you're not going to disappear in Iowa.

104 … By the time I got back to Stanley Hall, I had charged myself up to get it done. Some of the poems I had submitted could be resubmitted, but Deb, the woman in the Writers Workshop office, suggested I "swap *at least a few of them* out." She said, "I'm only saying this because I know who's reading the submissions. If they see the exact submission twice, you won't get in." I asked Deb for any other hints. She said, "I can't." I needed a quiet space to work, somewhere I could spread out. When I stepped into the lounge, I realized I couldn't work there. Andy had Shane in a wrestling hold on the floor. Shane's arms were being used to force his face against the carpet. Andy said, "Listen runt. I realize you like telling jokes. I like jokes. I tell a few once in a while myself. But, my mama ain't territory for yer walking. Are you picking up what I'm laying down?" Shane was very clear about how well he understood what Andy was saying. He grunted twice. "I'm picking it up."

105 ... I gathered what I could into my backpack, along with the Power-book, and ditched the Lounge. The library was pinched between Madison Street and the railroad tracks, a gargantuan brick building with long, slender windows. It looked like a giant bar code. I went to the first kiosk I found. The girl behind the counter had big bones and a round furry face. Pigtails or not, it would only get worse for her. She led me to a private study room where I got to work on the manuscript. It took some time, but I identified about twenty pieces and began pacing the room reading to myself, gesturing, performing in silence. One by one, I chiseled the *maybes* to eight pieces and ten pages. It was the best of what I could offer. A few of the poems were experimental, but the majority I thought revealed an awareness worth further consideration. I checked and rechecked my checklist and put everything into my backpack. Then, for the first time in a long time, I prayed.

106 ... I got back to the Lounge and all the guys were leaving, following Rugby. "What's up?" I said. "Party," Rugby answered. "You should come." I dropped my backpack in the Lounge and changed my shirt. A party was exactly what I needed. Apparently, it was what five-hundred other people needed too. The walk to the party was short. While everyone else from the lounge chummed it up. I was simply taking in the night, enjoying the weightlessness of having completed another challenge. The party was at a fraternity house. Rugby's entry fee was waved because he'd brought eight "potentials." We were each handed a white circle sticker with a black P. We were supposed to wear it. I put mine in my pocket. Behind the house was a fenced-in lot. The fence line and trees were lit with white Christmas lights. There was a sea of drunken underage coeds hiding from the Iowa City police. I found the keg and drank a beer with a guy wearing a P sticker. He thought I was a brother because I wasn't wearing a P sticker. He filled my plastic tumbler whenever I drank out of it. A few minutes later, I saw Rugby cutting through the crowd holding his

beer over his head. He was smiling. He was wearing an L sticker. "What's with the L?" I asked. "I'm a legacy," he said. "I'm already in. Follow me, I found some hash."

107 … There was a DJ in the living room and people dancing below a Delta Chi sign mounted to the wall above the fireplace. Rugby led me upstairs to a room labeled Gymnasium. He knocked in a coded way and opened the door to a living space, someone's bedroom. It was decorated in yellow and black. In one of the wings of the room was a loft bed and a couch. Sitting on couch in the corner was Honey's doppelganger. It was startling. I followed Rugby. He sat down on the couch, far from the girl. He said, "H, this is Karen. Karen, H." I shook her hand, but I couldn't keep my eyes off of her. Karen noticed. She asked Rugby, "What's with the savant?" I broke my stare and apologized, "You remind me of some- one. A friend. You could be twins." Karen said, "Lucky girl" and handed a ball of hash to Rugby. He smelled it and pulled the ball apart. We watched him string it out into a long thin line he handed to Karen. Karen sprinkled the long thin dowel with some shake and tobacco. Rugby showed me the blond crumbly hash in the palm of his hand and said, "*Hash.*" I told him I knew what it was. I didn't want Karen to think I was a complete idiot. "No," Rugby countered. "Your new name. *Hash.* It's better than Henry, don't you think?" Karen watched my reaction while she finished rolling the joint and said, "I like *H* more."

108 … The high moved through me like a long heavy snake. I continued to tell myself that I wasn't looking at Honey. It wasn't easy. Karen was tracing a pattern in the rug. I was mesmerized by her movements, the line

of her arm, the way her hair was draped. I felt like I was home again. Karen caught me staring more than once. "I have the wa-was," she said. "Let's get out of here." Rugby was sedate, but alert. He gave me a look as Karen took my hand and said, "Do what you want. *I'm* going to stick around." I told Rugby that I'd be back. The look he gave me suggested I wouldn't. Karen and I left the Delta house. I was following her, trying to keep up. Her apartment was on the second floor of a building around the corner. The key was above the door jam. "You didn't see that," Karen said. The place was small. It smelled like a girl. The tables and shelves and window-sills were decorated with painted sculptures expelling light. "Are those lamps?" I asked. "Amy's boyfriend is an artist. Amy's my roommate. Will you lock the door?" I made sure the door was closed and locked. By the time I turned around Karen had situated herself on the couch with a small box in front of her. "You want to do some coke?" I was pretty sure that I did. "Of course you do," she said. "You don't talk much, do you?" I told her I like watching. "The words come out much better when I'm writing." Karen sat down on the couch beside me and said, "Ah. You're one of those." I asked her what she meant. She tapped out an enormous pile of powder on a small mirror and said, "The *creative* type." I guess I was still lost in the hallucination, because I called her Honey when she handed me the coke and a straw. Maybe she thought it was a term of endearment. She said, "Take as much as you like, *dear*."

109 ... There was something special about Karen's coke. "Take another bump," Karen said. "You think you feel good now...." One bump at a time, my head swelled like a beehive. I don't remember who made the first move, but I do remember Karen's tongue. It was aggressive. She was assertive. One minute, we were making out. The next, we were arriving at the apex of our efforts on the floor near the door.

110 ... I slid the envelope with my poetry manuscript under the Writers Workshop door. It was late and getting early. The janitor was sweeping the halls with a dust mop. I avoided him enough to be seen, but not bother him. On my way back to the lounge, I walked along the river and watched the sunrise. Once I got accepted to the Writers Workshop, there was no stopping me. I was ready for anything. The first item on my list was sleep.

111 ... I laid down on my bed in the Lounge and I was out. The next thing I knew, Rugby was shaking my bunk. I hadn't been asleep very long. The lounge was starting to get hot. My mouth was as warm and aromatic as a compost heap. Large black flies were throwing their small bodies at the window. Rugby pushed my legs over and sat on the end of the bed. He was smiling. I had a headache of the severest kind. He was holding a bong. "Bong hit?" I told him I had class that morning. He wasn't taking *No* for an answer. "Haaaash, it's time to wake uhhhp." I realized it was the only thing that would make him go away. I put my feet on the floor and took the bong from him. I passed the lighter over the bud enough to ignite the crystals but not to scorch the weed, inhaling slowly to condense the smoke into a thick cloud that would somehow alter my future. I inhaled the smoke in a single catastrophic breath that expanded like a blow fish in my lungs and sent me choking, spitting, and hacking to the kitchenette sink. Anyone who was trying to sleep was now awake. I was burping smoke. My vision was strobing. The blackouts were almost audible. It took a while, but I was finally able to navigate the room. I managed to get dressed and find my student ID. I followed Rugby down the hall. Three of my five senses were set on random. The rest of me was in the wind. I was wearing sunglasses. Rugby stopped at a corkboard in one of the hallways and shouted, "Timothy Leary! Holy shit! That's this week!"

112 ... Rugby was in the middle of a discourse on cafeteria food. He handed me a tray and pointed at the pans of food behind the counter glass. "The only way I can eat this shit is if I get baked. There's something wrong with that. Look at the lard in those eggs." There was a very obvious layer of hardened shortening. The employees were offended and curious. "Dude, did you try the chicken fried steak these guys made last night? It was like deep-fried burlap. Maybe I'm getting spoiled. Delta has their own chefs." Rugby passed on most of the rest of the buffet. I got an unhealthy serving of bacon and made a Belgian waffle. Rugby found two chairs at a table with two girls and a quiet older fat guy. The girls were keeping to themselves. The big guy was shy. Rugby said, "How did it go with Karen last night?" He put a hunk of cheesecake in his mouth and laughed. "You just turned so red. Was it good? Was it sweaty?" The already curious diners at our table went silent. Rugby laughed, "Am I embarrassing you?" The girls were waiting for me to say the wrong thing. "She's nice." I said. Rugby laughed. "Nice? No she's not. She's a black widow. I'd be careful if I were you." I've opened my mouth and inserted my foot before. I wanted to wait until something clever came to me. Nothing did. The girls went back to whatever it was they were talking about. Rugby had an ear on their conversation. He spoke up. "Are you pledging Phi-Delt?" The girls said they were. Rugby said, "I'm a leg at Delta-Chi." Their demeanors changed. "Oh, a party boy," one of them said. "Are you a swimmer?" the other asked. "I'm a lifeguard," Rugby said, winking at me. "This is Hash. He's with me." One of the girls looked at the other and said, "What a cool name." The big guy had officially been crowded out. He picked up his tray and left. Then it was just the four of us.

113 ... Rugby burped and compared our schedules on the pedestrian path

behind Burge Hall. We had the same class that afternoon – Art of Rhetoric, "at the EPB." Other than that, we were going opposite directions. He walked backwards, pointing at me. "Think about pledging Delta. We've got the hook-ups!" I had thought about it. I wasn't pledging. I didn't need a gang. I wanted to be alone. I was willing to wait for privacy. Until then, however, I was willing to "Party on!"

114 … The walk to the Field House took longer than I expected. I was 10 minutes late to class. It didn't matter. It was Relaxation Techniques. The whole point of the class was to unwind. The room was a basketball court separated by a movable wall. I made eye contact with the instructor and she asked me my name. I found an open space on the floor and announced myself. Moments later, everyone spread out into a grid. We stretched and lightly exercised for 30 minutes and laid down on the floor for ten. This was our first technique. As simple and silly as it sounds, it was exactly what I needed.

115 … The Art of Rhetoric was going to be torture. The classroom was small and dark, on the second floor in the EPB. In the center of the room was a forty-something-year-old blond lady who was really a brunette, and a Russian exchange student with big breasts, copper hair, and a beautiful smile. She was talking to an Asian kid in mismatched clothes, splattered with paint. A very large woman and a very large man in sweatpants and t-shirts sat together in the back of the room. I was sure they were the fat couple I'd heard about. In front of them were two girls fresh out of high school and two older guys at the far end of the room. The old white guy looked like a truck driver. He was wearing a mesh baseball cap with a

bulldog hot-melted on the panel above the bill. The other guy was well dressed. There was a leather briefcase beside him. Rugby took a sharp left when we walked in and found a seat at the back wall. I sat next to him, beside a closet. A couple of minutes later the instructor came in. She was pale and dark with long dark hair and loose dark clothes. She looked over the room and set some things on the desk. She said, "My name is Annabelle. Yes, my last name is *Shady*. Contrary to what some of you may or may not have been told, we will not be meeting three times a week for 50-minute classes. We will be meeting for three hours on Monday nights only. The class runs for 17 weeks. There will be multiple essays and speaking and debating assignments which you will all be required to *complete* for a passing grade. I do not give A's unless your work is perfect and I do give F's where they are warranted. I will not be late, you are expected to be on time...." Rugby let out a grunt. "On that note," Miss Shady said. "Would you introduce yourself." Rugby didn't miss a beat. He said, "Sure! My name is Cole. I'm an alcoholic." Everyone laughed, except Miss Shady. She said, "My classroom is not a comedy club, Cole." Rugby apologized and offered his major as a consolation prize. Miss Shady pointed at me next. I only offered my name. Miss Shady suggested I say something more. I wanted to assure her that I was a competent student. I said, "I'm applying for the Writers Workshop." Miss Shady said, "Writing? That's not exactly a lucrative career. Wouldn't you rather be a biochemical engineer like Cole here?" She waited for me to respond, but I was taken aback. I knew there were other options. I just hadn't considered them. "I know," I said. "I have a problem."

116 ... By the end of Rhetoric class, I needed a smoke. Rugby and I went outside. He handed me a "European cigarette" – tobacco with hash. I put the cigarette to my mouth and the Asian kid from our class came out and lit the cigarette before I could. It was pure strange behavior. His name was G, but when he spelled it, it was much more confusing. He was flamboyantly excited, like some muscular dancer. He was all over the place, touching everything – the railing, the brick columns, my flannel shirt. "Isn't this

hot?" he laughed. But there was no space to answer. G said, "I've been meeting so many cool people! Who do you like to read? I mean, a writer! You probably know a ton of stuff!" G wasn't full of energy, he was energy. He smoked two cigarettes in the time it took Rugby and I to smoke the Euro-joint. "That's got a great aroma," G said. "What kind of tobacco is that?" Rugby answered him. "It's Dutch blond tobacco with a little blond Lebanese hash. Want some?" G looked at two of us and the roach and laughed. He said, "I've never had two blonds before. Hello metropolis!"

117 … G wanted to tell us everything all at once. He started out as a Business major at a college in Grinnell, Iowa, his hometown. By his own account, he shouldn't have been there. When he was six days old, some-one left him in a basket with a note at a police department somewhere in Korea. He was sent to an orphanage. One day, a white woman from America showed up. She wanted to adopt a child. He said, the nuns at the orphanage blindfolded her and put all the children in a circle. They spun her around until she was dizzy, then they told her to point to the child she wanted. She picked G. Now, he was on the fence. He wanted to pursue an art degree, but he still hadn't told his family. He was manic, wild, and expressive. When he asked for my phone number, I hesitated. I didn't want to seem rude, but I didn't really want to get to know the guy. I used the temporary housing scenario as a shield, but G wasn't taking *No* for an answer. He said, "Alright, mister Henry. This is for you. Call me any time! I'll see you guys next week!" G handed me a piece of paper with his phone number. And then he hugged me. As G walked away, Rugby said exactly what I was thinking. "Wow."

118 ... Before I went to sleep that night, I pinched the only photograph I had of Honey between the mattress and the metal supports on the underside of the top bunk. In an instant, I was transported to the moment I asked her to pose on the railing on the bow of the Sam Patch – a canal boat in Rochester – and snapped the photo. Her hair was in the wind. A storm was in her eyes. We were very drunk. The sun was going down. The lights of the city formed a gossamer half circle over the horizon. She smiled, but it was a smile of coriander. It took some prodding, but Honey trusted me. "When Nonnie (her grandmother) was sick, I went to visit her. The hospice nurse had an errand to run. I was baby-sitting, essentially." Honey paused. "Nonnie had this little porcelain bell she rang whenever she needed something. She asked me to open the window. It was cool outside, but sunny. The rose bush next to her window was blooming. I asked her if she needed anything else. She patted the bed for me to sit down. She was in so much pain. The tumor in her back was so large it had broken through the skin. Nonnie asked me for some water. I helped her drink. She asked for a sleeping pill and I helped her take it. Then she asked me for *more*." Honey's story stopped there. I asked her what she was saying. "You can do it," she said. "Kill," she added. "It's not hard."

119 ... I woke from a dream. One moment, I was standing at the edge of a lake. There were boats and docks and a forest of fir trees on fire. The lake was steaming. I was sweating gold. The scenery reminded me of Lake Massawepie, where I went to Boy Scout Camp. The next moment, I was in the Lounge. It was incredibly hot. I needed water, some moving air. The rest of the guys in the Lounge were laid out like invalids in the recovery ward of the hospital. I walked to the kitchenette. Justin had been supplying the lounge with dishes. The counter was stationed with empty Chinese food containers, plastic plates and utensils, plastic tumblers from gas stations, napkins from The Airliner, and hot sauce from Panchero's. I walked down the hall and filled an Iowa Hawkeye cup with water from the water fountain. It was cold. I wetted my hands, face and neck and made my way to the Stanley Hall kiosk. There was a young girl working. I asked her

for a fan, "For the third floor lounge? It's dangerously hot in there. There is zero circulation." She said there was nothing she could do, "We don't supply fans. Try a cold shower?" There was someone behind me. I stepped out of the way and went outside. All I could do was sit on the stoop.

120 ... Later that morning, I stopped by the credit union to check my finance box. I swiped my card and keyed in the pin number. When my balance appeared on screen, I laughed out loud. I'd never seen so much money in one place, sure a thousand dollars looks like a lot, but this was twenty times that. I knew they were credits. I knew I couldn't just take the money out whenever I wanted to. I had responsibilities now. I promised I would pay for my education with what I'd been loaned. "I shouldn't," try to take out "just a little." But I did.

121 ... Our Relaxation Technique instructor was walking between the rows of students. We positioned ourselves on small pillows around the exercise room. She was talking about meditation. She said, "Why don't we give it a try? Get comfortable. Cross your legs. Sit up straight. Place your hands in your lap. Take a deep breath. Exhale deeply. Again. Inhale. Inhale just a little more. Exhale. One more time. Like this." She inhaled deeply and exhaled slowly. "Again. We want to learn this rhythm of breathing. As we breathe in, we focus on our posture. On our legs, on our butts, on the arch of our back. As we breathe out, we adjust ourselves. We straighten our backs. We pull our shoulders back. We turn our chins down just a bit. This opens the airway completely. Breathe in. That's it. And out. I know some of you will want to close your eyes. But let's keep our eyes open. We are focusing on a single spot about two feet in front of us." There was

a girl in front of me. I looked at her ass. "And, return to your posture, the arch of your back, your chin is down, you are exhaling, focusing on the floor in front of you. As we breathe in, we focus on how we are breathing. We want the breath to be deep and refreshing. By keeping our eyes open, we are able to focus on our cycle of breathing. We begin and end on the spot of earth in front of us. Good. Your eyes are open. Your attention is on your posture. You are relaxed and focused on your breathing." There was a distinctive thump in the front of the room. The instructor jogged in the direction of the sound. A girl was rubbing her face, embarrassed. "Are you alright?" the instructor asked. "I fell asleep," the girl said. "I know," the instructor answered.

122 ... I was relaxed. I had a pocket full of cash and only one class that afternoon. The walk from east to west campus was slow. The heat was penetrating. The entrance to Stanley Hall was blocked. There were work-men replacing the doors. A detour sign led me to the front door of Currier Hall. There was new construction and an elevator, a telephone bank, old brass mailboxes, and a newly remodeled office or study room down one of the halls. The room was empty, very recently painted. The windows were open. There was a box fan in one of the corners, circulating the air. I could feel a gentle breeze and I closed my eyes. That gave me an idea. I walked over and unplugged the fan. A few minutes later, I was lying on my bed in the lounge with the fan in the window beside my bunk. I was looking at the photograph of Honey. I was happy. I hoped Honey was too.

123 ... My History of Relationships class was not what I expected. As the professor – a stout bowl-cut-and-bangs tomboy – introduced herself, I

realized three things: first, the subtext of the class was the role of women in the Catholic Church; second, I was one of two guys in a room with fifty women; third, a very attractive girl with short brown hair, sitting two seats over, was looking at the embroidered red daisy that Honey sewed on my shorts. The professor continued, "Over the course of the semester we'll be examining sixteen texts written by and about women who helped to modernize Church politics." I sighed out loud. I had the attention of my neighbors. I smiled and feigned interest but, I could have cared less. The girl a couple seats down leaned toward me and said, "Daisy." She pointed at the embroidered flower. "That's my name." Daisy was tan, spotted in freckles. Her eyes were faded jade. Class passed in a hot flash. When we were dismissed, I paced Daisy into the hall. She said, "We've met before." I told her *I have one of those faces.* "*Maybe*," she said. I must have rattled on about something because the next thing I knew, we were at the bike racks. Daisy threw her book bag over one shoulder and walked toward one of the bikes. She found a key on her key chain, smiled and said, "You know, you haven't even told me your name yet." I was absolutely distracted by her. She was stunning. I offered Daisy my full name, in an official manner, doing my best to disambiguate Nigh-teen. "Or," I said. "You can call me *Hash*?" Daisy stopped what she was doing and smiled. "Did you say *Hash*?"

124 ... I thought about Daisy on the way back to the Stanley Hall Lounge. A few of the guys were sitting around the table in the kitchenette. Something was wrong. Justin pointed to his leg. His knee was wrapped in a removable cast. There was a large plastic bag filled with ice slung over it like two packs on the back of a mule. "Torn ACL," Justin said. We all knew that football was the thing he was depending on. I asked him what happened. "Mike wasn't plugging the three hole ... I was Louie," Justin said. "Dwight came through and I nailed him. The line fell on us. I felt my leg bend backwards ..." Everyone winced. Justin said what was on everyone's mind. "The trainers are optimistic. I'm fucked."

125 ... The lounge telephone rang. The call was for me. I asked who it was. Shane said, "What am I your secretary?" I picked up the receiver. I didn't recognize the voice or the cadence. They were talking fast and loud. I had to pull the phone away from my ear to understand any of it. No one I knew had this kind of energy, except maybe "G?" G answered "YEAH!" I wanted to ask him how he got the telephone number, but that one question was all I got in. He just kept making random sweeping statements, connecting the dots on a horizon only G could see. Ideas were like ants leaving the anthill. One after another they swarmed themselves. I held the phone out and looked at it. G said, "Do you want to get a cup of coffee some time?" I figured that while I had the floor I should set myself up. "You know, I'm kinda booked ... I just got a job and I have a ton of classes and homework already. We'll catch up in Rhetoric," which I was now considering dropping, if only to get away from G. He asked if I was going to the Timothy Leary lecture. I said I didn't think so. "Oh, man. You can't miss Leary!" I didn't say anything. I couldn't. G was talking so fast that he interrupted himself. "All work and no play makes Henry an overworked underplayed boy with arms full of homework and ..." I'd had enough. I said, "I have to go, G. I'll see you in class. Okay. Bye." I don't think he heard me. I laid the phone on the receiver like it was a link of regurgitated sausage and unplugged the main line at the wall. I didn't want anything to do with the guy. G gave me the creeps.

126 ... I woke up hours later in my bunk bed. Rugby was moving some of his stuff around and packing. I sat up. Rugby was with one of the Delta brothers. He was moving into the Delta house. Rugby said, "Why move into a dorm room if I'm only going to move again, right? Did you get your

room assignment today?" I didn't know it, but the front desk was holding mail for those of us in temporary housing. I hurried down the hall, but there wasn't anything for me at the front desk. By the time I got back to the lounge, I had hatched a plan. I pitched the idea to Rugby. He seemed to think my calculations held a certain logic. He asked me to help him. Rugby and I carried his black trunk down the hall and set it on the floor near the front desk. Rugby's Delta brother, Paul, was holding the light stuff. Rugby laid out the scenario for the woman behind the counter while Paul and I talked. He said, "We're having another fund-raiser on Friday. You should come by. Karen will be there." It was enough to pique my attention. Rugby pointed at me and said, "This guy." The woman behind the counter said, "I can make it happen if both of you defer your room assignments." Rugby asked what we had to do. It was a simple change form. She handed Rugby a pen. Rugby held the pen over the signature line and read some of the fine print. Before signing, Rugby looked at me and said, "I'll do this on one condition." His room assignment was a single. After so many days and years spent with too many other people, I could finally be alone. I nodded emphatically. "Name it."

127 … Rugby wanted me to pledge the fraternity. I told him I would if he could convince me it was a good idea. "Sell me on it," I said. Something told me Rugby just wanted a friend to pledge with, someone to stand by or someone to outrun. I considered Rugby a friend, and I knew this was something he had to do. He was a legacy. His path was through the Delta family. It made me wonder what turned Dad away from masonry. For generations, it's what the men in my family did. My grandfather and his brothers and my great- and great-great grandfathers were all masons. Stone and mortar were in our physiology, our psyche. Maybe these text blocks are my way of building my own house. Maybe this is my own *proof of life*.

128 ... I was sitting on the railroad bridge looking south. The EPB was an unimpressive stack of bricks. The workshop would have the list up. I was nervous. What if I didn't get in? *What if* is a bad thing to think when you're on a railroad bridge. The water below was a reminder of that. Who knew how shallow it was, what nefarious scatterings might be below the surface? I got off the bridge and walked to the EPB and up the stairs to the fourth floor. Two guys were patting each other on the back in the hallway that led to the shabby Writers Workshop office. I scanned the list. Then I re-scanned it. "*Undergraduate Poetry Workshop*, right?" I looked at the other lists, "Prose" and "International." My name wasn't on any of them. I pulled the sheet of paper off the corkboard and walked in the office. Deb, the office manager, looked it over, pressed her lips tight and prepared the following words. "You're right. I *don't* see your name."

129 ... I was a wind storm. No one else was in the lounge. I went off, shaking my bunk, stomping, shouting. "What the fuck!" I had no interest in Iowa if I wasn't going to be in the Writers Workshop. None. I needed to get the hell out of there. Iowa was a hot box along the steaming river and I was trapped. The lounge was spinning, in aura. I was going to have a seizure. I didn't care. I prayed it was the one that would take me. The wall went up like a curtain. I don't know if hours or seconds passed. I've traveled dimensions in the closing of my eyes. I woke some time in the future, on the carpet. The right side of my face was throbbing. I was exhausted, sore from cramping. I rolled over and watched the bottoms of the curtains sway from time to time. There was little that attached itself to words. I found my way to a chair. The next thing I realized, someone was standing over me. A strange woman. She looked like a librarian. She said, "I'm looking for Henry." I was slow to understand. She repeated herself. "I'm Henry," I said. She handed me a small envelope marked with a key inside. "This is your room key. You can move in tomorrow. Sign here."

130 ... Rugby came by the lounge to get the last of his things. He saw how fucked up I was. I told him about the Workshop. He took it lightly. He said, "So what?" I repeated, "*So what?*" He said, "Are you going to let *that* define you?" I had gone over it in my head ten times the power of uncertainty. *Maybe* writing wasn't my *thing*. "Here," Rugby said. He opened one of his boxes and gave me a wood sculpture of a hand with the middle finger extended. I told him he didn't need to give me the finger. "Think of it as a reminder," he said. "Fuck 'em. You want to be a writer? *Fucking write.*"

131 ... Rugby was right. It was up to me to define my life. I went to breakfast in the Burge cafeteria. I was focused on turning this negative into a positive. I had a bowl of cereal and a cup of coffee and opened the Daily Iowan – the university's newspaper. I wasn't reading the stories, just the headlines. There was an ad for the Academic Advisors Office at the bottom of one of the pages. That's where I needed to go. They would know what to do. I finished eating and found their office on the third floor of the EPB. I waited in the lobby of the English office for my advisor to finish another meeting. My advisor was a very large woman in a small office. A beast in a cave. She called me into her office. The furniture arrangement left little room for personal space. She was sweating, one-hundred-fifty pounds overweight. The top few buttons on her blouse were undone and a number of long black hairs curled from between her sagging, pock-marked breasts. Her upper lip was carpeted in coarse bleached yellow hair. Each of her eyes seemed to have a separate focus. She pulled a pen from behind her ear and crowded me. She was holding my class schedule. "Why are you

only taking three courses this semester, Henry? And what in God's name is *Relaxation Technique?*" Before I could answer, she said, "Relationships? Rhetoric? When do you plan to graduate? 2050?" I wasn't sure she was done, but she was staring. I said, "You don't have to be rude." What did I care? She was no one to me. She stopped fidgeting. She almost stopped sweating. She got angry with me. She asked me what I wanted to do with my life. The answer came effortlessly. "I'm a writer." She repeated my answer, adding, "How rewarding. Have you entered an application to the Writer's Workshop?" I told her in as few words as possible that I had been rejected. She said, "Listen, Henry. This is college. There is no shortage of opportunity. Obviously you're here for a reason. You must be a smart kid." She looked at a chart in my file. "Yes. It says here you're a smart boy." She continued turning pages in my file. She said, "You have 48 credits transferring from RIT ... but I don't see any foreign languages. You need four semesters of a language to graduate." I'd always opted for literature electives over languages, it was a habit more than anything. I remembered in that moment that Honey studied French in high school. "What about French?" I asked. "It's a start," she answered.

132 ... I loaded my things on a cart that I would wheel to my new room the next morning. Leaving Rochester, I unburdened myself with anything that meant less to me than the writing and the few items I'd collected in my posterity box. It kills me that so many of these personal effects remain unattended, unprotected at Currier Hall in room N333. But I wasn't there yet. Nor am I there now. Once everything was packed, I went to Burge for dinner and to the Delta house for dessert. Rugby answered the door. "*Hash!*" There was a circular sheet of plastic on the floor in the foyer. "Oh, hey, watch that. We painted the crest on the floor today. You want a beer or something?" I told Rugby I'd take the "or something. What do you have?"

133 … Rugby was a natural salesman. He said, "One of the best things about Delta is our ability to find and tap essential resources. If you need a tutor, we'll find you the best tutor on campus. If you need a date for a social engagement, we've got you covered. You need a job, an internship, toys, furniture, tickets to a football game, emergency cash … there's nothing we can't do, or help you do, *if you're one of us*." Rugby led me to the main kitchen. He opened one of the refrigerators. It was marked with Greek letters. I asked him what it said. Rugby looked around then whispered, "Brothers only." The fridge was large enough to fit two bodies. There were cases and bottles of beer. Fixed to the inside of the door were several beer taps. Rugby poured a black and tan using two of the taps. He closed the fridge and opened a cabinet. The shelves were lined with bottles of whisky, rum, vodka, gin, tequila, mixers and barware. "Tequila?" he asked. "Tequila," I said. Rugby handed me a small cutting board, a few limes and led me upstairs with the bottle of tequila and his black and tan. Where the main floor mocked the second floor in style, the upstairs humiliated the former in temperature. "Jesus man, I figured you guys would have air conditioning." Rugby said, "That's what the fund-raisers are for. We're saving to replace our air conditioner. Here's my room." He had moved into the Gymnasium. It was a great room, almost the size of the third-floor lounge at Stanley Hall. The two beds were lofted, the ceiling had multiple angles. The rest of the room was laid out like an apartment, decorated with drinking signs, posters of classic Rock-n-Roll musicians, a dart board with blow darts deeply fixed in the cork. The couch was flanked by an Iowa Hawkeye flag and two enormous stereo speakers. Rugby opened the windows to get some airflow. The windows opened onto the street. Rugby ducked back inside. Someone on the street called his name. "Shit," he said, positioning himself back in the window. "Hey, what's happening *Karen*?"

134 ... Rugby and I winced from the tequila shots and sucked on slices of lime, as someone knocked a special knock. "Clear!" Rugby shouted. Delta brother Paul came into the Gymnasium and paused as he started to say something. "Is that a black and tan?" he said. Rugby tried to hide the beer. Paul came closer. "Is that my tequila? That shit's like two-hundred bucks a bottle, man! Oh, hell no." Rugby tried to explain himself. It wasn't working. Paul said, "Follow me. You too." Paul pointed at me. Rugby looked at me and said, "I'm sorry man." Rugby followed Paul. I followed Rugby. Paul led us to the kitchen – where we had gotten the black and tan and the tequila – announcing "Punishment" as we went. It wasn't long before we had an audience. Paul positioned himself across the counter from Rugby. He asked Rugby to explain the circumstances of his impending punishment "loud enough so everyone can hear you clearly." Rugby told everyone what I just told you. I felt bad. The brother looked at me and said, "Because you aren't officially a pledge, I have no authority over you. You, however," he said to Rugby, "are a different story. You are a legacy. You should know better. You *do not* circumvent the route to brotherhood *in any way*! You've broken two rules tonight." The brother reached into a cupboard and pulled out a bag of onions. He looked Rugby in the eye and said, "Eat." Rugby laughed. "You want me to eat an onion?" Paul smiled and pushed the bag across the counter. "I want you to eat all of them." Rugby took a breath. Someone said, "That'll kill him." Rugby asked if he had to eat the skins or the root ends. Paul said he could "clean them up" before eating them. "Thank you, sir. Can I pour you a black and tan, sir? Watching you enjoy the beer while I take my punishment might help me remember this valuable lesson." Paul agreed and Rugby poured a perfect black and tan. He offered Paul the beer with an additional apology. Then, one by one, Rugby prepared thirteen onions and ate them like apples. The smell alone brought everyone in the kitchen to tears. Some of the brothers and pledges had to leave it was so bad. Paul watched quietly, sipping the black and tan in one of the far corners of the kitchen. Occasionally, Paul asked Rugby to repeat a point of interest in Delta's "long history." Rugby nailed every question while coughing, choking, weeping and sweating. I had to back away from him, but I stayed. Before Paul left the kitchen, he pointed at me and said, "I'm not done with you."

135 … Rugby laid down on the Gymnasium floor and hugged a Hawkeye trash can. Karen was sitting on the couch beside Paul. Her skin was red-turning-plum. She said she'd been outside all day, in the sun. Paul took a bong hit. He was smiling, enjoying the wreckage he had caused Rugby. Karen was getting irritated by Rugby's retching. She got up and asked me to follow her outside for a cigarette. She took my arm. We went out front. She lit a cigarette. She said, "Paul isn't always this mean. He can be really … sweet." I wasn't interested in Paul. He was a bully, but I wasn't going to bitch about it. Rugby's problems were his problems. "Everyone chooses their choices," I said, looking into Karen's eyes. Her pupils were dilated. I asked her, "What's in the thermos?" She said it was tea. "Want some?" She poured me a capful. The tea was psilocybin. It tasted like dirt and vinegar but when you know what's on the other end, you don't care. "Aren't you going to have some?" I asked. "No," Karen said, "I already had some. Then I had some more."

136 … Karen dangled some keys and said her car was up the street, near the Dey House. The heat had waned. The streetlights and dorm lights were nerves of energy. Karen was fiddling with a flower, keeping to herself, walking ahead of me. Our conversations were like weighted dice, they fell where Karen wanted them to. She walked up the steps and into Currier Hall. I said, "What are we doing here?" She said, "It's this way." She kept pace down a long hallway, past an elevated vending machine area. I stopped and asked her if she was thirsty. I reached into my pocket and slipped my groover in and out of the dollar slot on the soda machine. The soda arrived in a thud. Karen was stunned. Did I really have a dollar attached to a strip of tape? She wanted to see it. She wanted to use it. I told her she hadn't seen anything. The mushrooms took over then. Walk-

ing through the basement of the old cavernous dormitory was an adventureland. Echoes of elevators and generators and hot water boiler motors were layered in reverberating loops you could feel if you touched the cold cement walls. Karen said, "It's like we're in the belly of a concrete monster." As we held our ears to the wall, listening to the building groan, a student wearing a beard and a backpack opened a set of large metal doors. It scared the hell out of us. We could see the exit sign at the end of the hall. We laughed and burst through the exit door and ran out into the parking lot. We were free again. Karen pointed to a car. "There it is." She held the keys and said, "You drive."

137 ... The mushrooms were effectively in control. The Riatta was a spaceship. The console was contoured and contorting. The dashboard lights were green. The stereo was a touchpad. Karen was somewhere between the passenger seat and eternity, curling her hair, telling me which way to go. Writers Workshop or not, it was all adding up. Karen laughed out loud and said, "Look, look." Someone was streaking across the Old Capital lawn. Our trajectories were coinciding perfectly. At the light on Iowa Avenue, I recognized the streaker. It was "G!" To be clear, G was naked, wearing dress boots, in a calm sprint. "I know that guy!" I said, honking. G turned toward the shadows. Karen and I were trying like hell not to laugh our way into an accident. Karen directed the car down Iowa Avenue, then left again at Dubuque. We went down the hill and were soon, effectively, off-campus. She changed the music and sang as we passed Mayflower Hall, snapping her fingers as we passed Interstate 80. Miles into a valley of trees, Karen said "Slow down. Turn here. Do you want to go swimming?" I turned into a wooded area. It was a dirt road. She knew exactly where we were going. "Park there. Turn the engine off. Leave the lights on." We got out. "Get undressed," she said. "Are you going to get undressed?" I asked. "You first. I have my period," she said. "I don't want you to see my pad." The crickets were singing. The lights from Iowa City formed a broad orange dome on the horizon. "Where's the water?" I asked, finally dropping my shorts. "Turn around," Karen said. It was

as if the lake had snuck up on me. I walked into the water. There was a cold undertow. The darkness shifted the further I went out. "It's nice," I said. "I'm sure it is," Karen said. The headlights were terribly bright. I said, "Why don't you kill the lights? Come on in." I was waist-deep in the water. Karen said, "You know, while I have you here, I should give you a message from Paul." I asked Karen what that asshole had to do with anything. Karen said, "Have a nice night," and she got into the Riatta. She started the engine. I shouted after her and ran through the water, but Karen wasn't stopping. By the time I got back to the beach the dust had settled on my shoes. Karen had my clothes. She had my ego. Once this got out, my reputation was dust. I picked up my shoes and said, "Looks like G's not the only one streaking tonight."

138 ... I knew if I followed the river, I'd end up back in town. I was sure the road would get me there too. I followed the tree line, stayed in the shadows. It wasn't easy, but I found Interstate 80 and the north edge of campus. I found the bike path and the stairs up to Stanley Hall. There was a light on in the Lounge. I threw a rock at the window. Andy and Shane came to the window. I said, "Throw me something to wear!" They were laughing their asses off as my "Good Luck" shirt and a pair of shorts floated down. At least the Lounge was safe. It was somewhere I could be angry. Everyone wanted to know the specifics of what happened. I just wanted to forget about it, and let the mushrooms take me deep into the future. It was everyone's last night in temporary housing. We had all been given our room assignments and we were going in different directions. Everyone had pitched in for cold beer and fast food, sodas and rolling tobacco. They were in high spirits and I was reliving my downer in the corner. When Shaquim showed up with Chinese, I decided to join the party. What could I do? It wasn't the first time I'd let a girl get the best of me.

139 … Rugby found me in the cafeteria the next morning. He apologized for what happened. "Karen is Paul's girlfriend." I had pieced some things together, but I told him about the coke and the sex. Rugby said, "Karen does whatever Paul says. Paul told her to fuck you. She ditched you because Paul told her to ditch you. She's the worst kind of girl. She's putty. *Fuck her* … anyway … if you still want in, you're in. I promise, pledging will be smooth sailing from here on out." I wasn't interested in pledging Delta. I wasn't even sure I was going to stick around. I was daydreaming about finding a quiet place to write, somewhere out west. I was thinking Hollywood would be a place to make my dreams come true. All I had to do was get there. I had enough cash to live where I wanted, thanks to the government loans. Rugby could sense my hesitancy. He took a piece of my bacon. "Think about it," he said, pointing at my food tray. "What's good this morning?"

140 … French class. The desks were in a circle against the walls. Everyone was seated. The instructor – a woman with frizzy blond hair and round thick eyeglasses – was teaching from the center. She adjusted her glasses and clasped her hands at her chest. "*Bon jour monsieur.*" The rest of it was French. "Sorry I'm late," I said. The instructor spoke in French. "I'm sorry," I said. "I don't know what you're saying." She giggled and said something else in French. My classmates smiled. I wondered if this was how I should be spending my second chance, my new life, my anonymity, being stared at by a bunch of Francophones. The instructor said, "I, am *Virginnie*" and she addressed the other students. One by one they said their names and the phrase *je m'appelle*. "Ça va," Virginnie said, "Je m'appelle Virginnie. Comment vous appellez-vous?" She wanted me to repeat the phrase I'd heard around the room. She wanted me to speak French. I said, "*Je m'appelle* Henry." Virginnie seemed impressed with the way I teased the phrase. She said, "E voila. Henri! You are in the right place. Why don't

you have a seat."

141 ... The rest of French class was white noise. There was a lot of homework that I would have to catch up on, but I forgot about it during my
Relaxation Techniques class at the Field House. We learned about yoga
and then stretched a little. After Relaxation Techniques I made my way
to Currier Hall, the third floor, North end. I followed the numbers toward
the music, past dorm room after dorm room, toward an exit sign. The door
was the second to the last on the left. It was marked with a small plaque
and the room number. There was a green construction paper balloon taped
to the door. It read, "Welcome to N333 Nick!" I used the key to open the
heavy metal door. The now-very-expensive-storage-room was small, with
a closet immediately to the right, a corkboard to the left, a sink and a mir-
rored cabinet combo on the room-side wall of the closet, high ceilings, a
bed and dresser, a bookshelf, a desk and a chair, a lamp, a telephone and a
binder of health and safety services. The floor was hard brown and green
tile. The walls, thick, hollow concrete. There was a large window overlooking a courtyard at the far end of the room. Below the window was a
steam furnace. It was the most wonderful place in the world. But it was
hot. Heavy. A tomb. I opened the window and leaned out for some fresh
air. There were three guys playing Frisbee in the courtyard. The view
was a breath of fresh air. I could and can imagine myself, leaning out the
window just far enough to fly. But this was no time to rest. I had to get
the moving cart back to the front desk by noon. I went to the Stanley Hall
Lounge and got my things. The whole moving process took some blood,
sweat and cursing but it was done. My clothes were put away, my personal
effects were stowed in drawers, and my new bed was layered in blankets I
would not need. I chewed a piece of gum and used it to stick Honey's picture to the wall above my bed. It felt incredible to be alone, to be human,
to have a place I could call my own. I looked at the picture of Honey on
the Sam Patch. I imagined her mouth, touching me. Then I closed my eyes
and disassociated myself from the act.

142 ... I fell asleep. I could have slept for days, dreamed in real time the formation of mountains, but someone was pounding on the door. They sounded angry. I opened the door. It was Rugby. He walked in and sat down at the desk. "Let's do this!" I wasn't sure what he was talking about. "Leary, man. The lecture is tonight! Nice place, by the way. You need some shit on your walls, but this could work." I had forgotten. "Don't we have Rhetoric?" Rugby scoffed, and asked if I had a towel. "Over there, top drawer." Rugby went to the drawer and opened it. He said, "Fuck Rhetoric." He rolled up a towel and dropped it along the bottom of the door jam and locked the door. Then Rugby went to the window, turned the fan around, and stuffed my pillow next to the fan to fill up the rest of the space. "What are you doing?" I asked. Rugby revealed a joint and a lighter. He lit the lighter and the joint. The gigantic flame pulled toward the window. He said, "We're gonna smoke this, I'm ventilating." By turning the fan around in the window he had created a wind tunnel. Air was coming in from around the door. All the smoke was getting sucked outside. It was pure, "Genius."

143 ... We were so high when we left N333 that our cheeks and eyes were swollen with shock. We walked down the hall in stunned silence. The elevator doors opened. A bunch of young girls with braces and bare arms, tan legs and jewelry, stopped laughing. Rugby said, "Ladies," as we entered. Someone had bathed in perfume. Rugby was smiling. The doors closed. Rugby said, "This dope has some pep to it." One of the girls giggled. The doors opened. We got the hell out of there. We walked toward Stanley Hall and down a long flight of stairs between the basketball courts and the Chemistry building. He said, "We're meeting at the Union." I

asked who we were meeting. "Not Paul and Karen?" I stopped. "Oh, come on," he said. "He's my roommate and he's the president of the fraternity. Don't hold a grudge. It's business, it's not personal. Dude, one of the other pledges ... they hid his car. He's been going around all week goin' Dude, where's my car? Another guy got his record collection glued together. The brothers test you. They have to. You have to want it. You have to let it roll off your back, man. Loosen up. You're waaay too tense some times." I thought I was pretty loose. I thought I was letting things roll off my back. But now that he mentioned it, Rugby had another point. Revenge is best served cold.

144 ... The Student Union was swarming with people looking for tickets to Timothy Leary's lecture. It was sold out. I saw Daisy – from my History of Relationships class – and stopped briefly to say hello. She was with several guys and girls. All of us were high. They had tickets. Even G had a ticket. It looked like G was plugged into something. There was an uncontrolled energy about him. He offered to let Rugby and I cut in line but we weren't getting the go-ahead from the people behind G. Rugby spotted Karen. Karen was alone. "Where's Paul," Rugby shouted. "Fuck Paul," Karen said. The line wasn't moving. Rugby and I left G to find out more. Karen said, "Paul went to the Foxhead. You know what? Screw this. Follow me." Karen led Rugby and I around the corner of the Student Union and in a side entrance. We found the front of the line leading to the Main Ballroom where Leary was going to speak. The line was moving but it broke into a mob. The lecture wasn't sold out. It was over-sold. There were a few hundred people with tickets and no space in the ballroom. Security was too thin to hold everyone back. Some people got through, but one gigantic guard after another filled in the frame of the ballroom doors and stopped us before we made it in. Karen attempted to seduce entry, but the guards shooed her away. The crowd dispersed. That was that. Rugby said, "I feel like I'm walking away from the chance of a lifetime." Karen said, "I know another way," but Rugby was already onto the next thing. He said, "I'm going to the Foxhead." He asked me if I wanted to go with

him. I wanted to see Leary. I asked Karen if she really knew a way. Karen seemed to think so. Rugby picked up on my body language. "Alright man, don't say I didn't *warn* you." Karen picked up on what he was insinuating. "Fuck you, Rugby." Rugby walked away. "No thanks," he said. "I heard you have crabs."

145 ... Karen led me through a few small corridors and down a short hall, through a miniature cafeteria to a set of doors blocked by stacks of chairs. "Ah, ha," Karen said. We had to move the chairs to get through the doors. We did it quietly. The doors opened to a dark room. One of the walls was framed in glass. They were doors. There was light and laughter coming from the other room. Karen pointed. I couldn't make out what she was pointing at. We moved closer and looked through the curtains. We were behind the stage. Timothy Leary was at a podium. He was speaking to the audience. His back was turned to us. Someone was heckling him. Karen leaned close to me and whispered, "I'm sorry about the other night. I *had* to do that." I said she didn't have to do anything. She said, "Paul pays my rent. I kinda did." I didn't offer absolution. We didn't have a chance to discuss it. A security guard shined his flashlight on us from the cafeteria doors where we came through. "You two," he said. "Get over here."

146 ... "I don't respect authority," Karen said. "It's a problem. That security guard got what he had coming. He was being a dick!" She had a cut and a bruise on her jaw from when the security guard wrestled her grip from his jacket. I didn't care that he kicked us out. I had seen Leary. Okay, I saw his ass, his backside, but it was still him. I opened the door to N333 and turned the light on. Karen went to the mirror and said, "Look at

this, I'm suing!" I teased her, "Contrary to what people think, you should *always* act out of emotion." Karen looked at me in the reflection of the mirror and said, "Now *you're* being a dick." I assured her, she hadn't seen the worst of it. Karen turned around and said, "You know, you come off as this geeky know-it-all, but a lot of people think you're full of shit." I was unconcerned what Karen or the Delta crowd thought. I said, "I don't care. I'm not sticking around." Karen suddenly seemed interested. "What do you mean? Where are *you* going?" she scoffed and tended to her face. "Hollywood," I said. "Hollywood?" Karen repeated. "Hollywood," I said.

147 … I hadn't unloaded on anyone in a long time. I told Karen everything, birth to if-I-died-standing-there. Every word of it was the truth, but Karen said, "I don't believe you." That's life, right? Lies and disbelief free us from knowing anyone intimately. Somewhere there was a hidden truth. Karen moved closer. She leaned in for a kiss. "I don't know if I can trust you," she said. "And that makes you want to kiss me?" I asked. "No," Karen said. "It makes me want to fuck you." I asked her about "the crabs" Rugby mentioned. She was confident, calm. "Rugby is full of shit." That was good enough for me. Karen guided me around the bases, then she went to her purse. I thought she was going to get a condom or a hair tie or something. She turned around with a small vile of white powder and a long thin stick in her hands. She sat down on the edge of the bed and inserted one end of the stick into the vile. "Want a bump?" she said, taking a little white pile into her head. She said, "Sex and heroin. Nothing better." I had never tried heroin. I took the bump. It was an incredible high from such a small amount of powder. By the time I realized it, Karen had me inside her. We tried a few positions, but the small bed made it difficult to get comfortable. Nothing was helping. When I looked her in the eyes, I saw Honey, I felt emasculated, cheated, vulnerable. I told her too much. I was losing it. Karen asked if everything was all right. I carried her to the top of the desk and said, "This will be better." There was *almost* nothing left to give.

148 ... I was dreaming, trapped, staggering, senseless. The telephone was ringing. I reached for it, but realized in free fall that I didn't have my footing. The floor was going to leave a bruise or two. We met like old foes. The telephone stopped ringing. I looked at the clock. I was late. It was training day at the Bagel Shop. I pulled on my khaki pants and the red polo shirt the manager gave me and drank a glass of warm lemonade made with tap water. I was nauseous by the time I reached the elevator. I walked to Iowa Avenue. The city was waking, silent as a bee hive. I didn't want to work. I didn't have to, especially if I was going to run with the money the government gave me. But I was there, at the front door. I clapped on the glass like a cop, an angry neighbor, a landlord. A small, short brown-haired fellow opened the door. "Henry? Hi. I'm Jon." He was in a panic. His baby had been up late. He over slept. He'd only walked in moments before I did. Nothing was ready. The oven wasn't even hot yet. He was unshaven. He had thick eyebrows and a small squashed face. He immediately went into training mode, starting with the basics. I kept pace with him through the prep area, to the walk-in, donning an apron and the tan baseball cap he handed me. He was retracing his steps every few points. It was distracting, even for me. But, there was an opportunity here. I told Jon that I had worked at the Bagel Shop in Rochester, that we could skip the intro and he could just put me to work. Jon sighed and said, "Really? What a relief! I hate training days."

149 ... Jon asked me to make "two bakers of each." There were cards on the wall with bagel flavors and recipes – poppy, pumpernickel, cinnamon-raisin, wheat, egg, blueberry, oat nut, asiago, onion, salt, and plain. Jon was on prep, bringing items from the walk-in to the reach-in up front.

Every time he brought something by the baking station, Jon would lay some little factoid or joke on me. I would chuckle or confirm interest and go back to daydreaming about my bank account, imaginary drugs and hookers in Hollywood, writing a screenplay, making a movie, becoming famous. The bagels had all been proofed the night before, so all I had to do was drop them in the rolling water for two minutes and lay them on the rotisserie baking racks until they were light brown. While the bagels baked, I weighed out the back ups of cream cheese, tomatoes, lettuce, sprouts, mayonnaise, mustard, oils and vinegars. I dropped two soups into a water bath to thaw and I shook the finishings on the bagels, delivering them to the warming baskets out front. Jon made coffee and counted the till. Then, like clockwork, the rest of the staff walked on stage five minutes before Jon opened the door for his regulars. Waiting on the laborer's side of the counter for the first order, Jon said, "It's going to be nice having you around, Henry."

150 … My colleagues at the Bagel Shop were the sweetest morons around. Luiza was beautiful but with a hair-lip and dark sultry eyes. Jeremy was a big guy and dumb. His shoelaces were untied. He was the mid-morning to mid-afternoon baker. He was very quiet, but precise and calm, cordial but not friendly. Carmen was the stout romantic wife with children. She worked the cash register. She was asking me all kinds of questions, a real chatterbox. She'd never been out of Iowa. I wondered if I could ever go home. It was distracting. I cut myself with a serrated knife while working on some guy's sandwich. Jon saw me fishing through the first aid kit and sent me on break when I got the bleeding under control. I walked up the street and bought a cigarette for 15 cents at City News. There was a pay phone on the sidewalk. I had Dad's calling card. I dialed Honey. Jean picked up on the second ring. "Honey? Is that you?"

151 ... Jean was in a panic. How was I supposed to know where Honey was? I'd been in Iowa for almost two weeks. I hadn't spoken with Honey since I left Rochester. It was a little worrisome, but I was brewing a fresh pot of dark roast, taking solace in the aromas. The Bagel Shop was promoting the fact that it brewed a pot of coffee every thirty minutes. The Bagel Shop had posters with little bakers taming giant cups of coffee with clocks on them. I changed the time on the brew-card that hung on the coffee carafe when the machine beeped. Moments later a tiny man with a giant Bagel Shop mug approached the counter. I had to look down at him, it was simple physics. I didn't intend to make him feel small. "When was the dark roast brewed?" he asked. I said, "I just completed the cycle" and offered to rinse and fill his mug. He said, "Maybe you did, maybe you didn't." I repeated myself. He said, "How do I know you're not lying? I don't believe you. I want you to make another pot. Make it now."

152 ... I honestly wish I had done more. Some people just need a beat down once in a while. I was sitting in Jon's office, wringing my apron, re-playing the scene. I said, "Sir, the coffee is so fresh I don't think it's even had time to realize it's coffee yet." It was a little snide, but I smiled and it was really meant to lighten the moment. Jon was writing all this down. "The guy said, Listen punk. You're going to dump that pot of coffee and make a new one, or I'm going to call your manager. I told him that he was going to have to trust me and I told him I didn't appreciate his tone. I was firm *and* professional. I wasn't rude. I told him that he was welcome to have the coffee I had just made or he could wait another half hour for me to make another pot. He said, 'I want you to make a new god-damned pot of dark roast, right-fucking-now.' That's when you came in. You heard him call me a half-wit and a retard. I saw the look on your face. That's when I quit." I climbed over the counter in my Bagel Shop apron and confronted the little man. I smacked the mug out of his hand and said, "Now what?"

Jon ran from behind the counter and stepped between us. He was right. I didn't want to hurt anyone, especially not over a pot of coffee. I was just upset about Honey. Pissed at myself. All I wanted was a little control over something. I wanted something real to hold onto, something I could destroy – if I wanted to.

153 ... Jon gave me the rest of the week off. I bought another few cigarettes at City News and went back to N333. I lit a cigarette and picked up the phone to call Honey. The phone wasn't working. A recording repeated a message. I needed a code to make a long distance call. I hung up and dialed 0. The operator answered. I asked about the code. She suggested I call the front desk. The only front desk I knew about was in Stanley Hall. I asked if she could connect me. When someone picked up, I posed the question and was put on hold. When she came back online she gave me a code to use my phone and said, "One more thing. You have some mail here. Do you want to pick it up?" I asked if it looked important. She said it looked "personal," and that the office was closing for the day. I could pick it up or come by in the morning. I stubbed out the cigarette and went right down. It was a bundle, in a box. The woman I spoke to on the phone looked nothing like I imagined. She was short, squat, thick and soft. She said, "Sorry about all the confusion. We had you registered, but we didn't know where you were. There have been a lot of problems this year. We'll forward everything to the mailbox for N333 starting tomorrow." She reminded me where the mailboxes were as I rifled through the box. There was a manila envelope from Dad and several small envelopes from Honey. All of Honey's envelopes were decorated with pearls of black hearts.

154 … I started with the oldest letter, the one Honey mailed first.

H,   I just got back from your house. I'm sorry I missed you. When I got home last night I was really drunk and I stayed up all night making you this mix-tape for your trip to Iowa, but I overslept. By the time I got to your place this morning, you had already left. The house was so empty looking. I am going to miss you, but I'm happy that you have something you love so much that you would leave everything you know to chase after it. No, actually, it sucks. I wish you liked me that much :^J. I know you'll be back at Christmas, but I wish it wasn't so far away. Wow, Iowa. Will you have any classes in barns? Are there lots of cows? You should have someone take a picture of you with a cow and send it to me. That would be cool. We should send each other lots of things and then when we're older we can look at those things and remember the cool stuff we did together. Like this tape. I know you probably won't know all the songs, but they mean a lot to me. They remind me of you and things we've done together. James too. I love you Henry. Are you listening to the tape yet? It's pretty awesome.

The cassette was wrapped in Christmas paper turned inside out. The white background was 'wrapped' in beads of black circles. The cassette cover art was a line drawing of the shape of New York and a tiny car riding a string of black beads to the shape of Iowa. Two stick figures were waving from the car windows. One of them had a beard, like Dad, the other wore a baseball cap. I inserted the cassette into my modest radio and pressed the play button. There was a lot of hissing and banging, then Honey's voice. She said, "Um. Testing? One-two? Okay. So, Henry, you're on your way to Iowa. We're going to miss you. I'm going to miss you. But this isn't goodbye. This is sweet music! Brought to you by Honey Rider!" I re-wound the tape to hear her voice again. There was a mountain of desire in my heart for her. A chunk of it chipped off and fell into the valley of my core, a dust cloud rising into my face as the music began – *The Dangerous Type*, by The Cars. While the music played, I looked through the envelopes for the next postmark date.

155 ... H,   *Did you get the mix-tape I made? I saw your dad today. He gave me a different address than the one I had when you left. I hope you got the tape, I spent a lot of time on it. I'm surprised I haven't heard from you yet. I guess you're probably distracted. Your dad said there are lots of pretty girls there. Who'da thunk it? Iowa girls pretty? You'll just have to take a lot of cold showers I guess! That will help you cool down. If you were here, you could swim in the pool. You could cannonball off the roof! My parents aren't home. They went to the boat. They invited me to go hang out with them, but it's way too small for the three of us. I stayed home and made muffin-cakes for Rufus' birthday. Raine and Lees came over and we sang happy birthday to Rufus. He had a little pink cone hat on. He couldn't blow out the candle, so we did it for him. He liked the muffin-cakes though. He had two! Raine and Lees were being weird. Just between me and you, I think they're doing heroin. They look like zombies. Raine has these marks on his arm. He said they're mosquito bites, but I didn't even ask what they were. When we went outside to have a cigarette on the porch, I noticed that Lees had the same marks on her feet. Weird, huh? I hope they're not doing that. That wouldn't be cool. I don't want them to end up all fucked up in a tenement with buckets catching the rain, you know. They're smarter than that. It was good to see someone though. I feel like I've been cooped up in the house since you left. When you come home at Christmas, we're going to have a party. I'll make something yummy. Are you coming home for Thanksgiving? You should call me. I have a lot of questions and you're not writing any answers. Where are you H? I hope you got the tape and letter. If you didn't get it, maybe it'll come back to me and I'll send it again.*

156 ... H,   *I wish you were here. When Raine and Lees were over the other night, they stole one of my mom's necklaces. Dad freaked. He got all of his detective buddies over here and they finger printed the room. Now I'm in trouble with them too. They grounded me for a week. What am I twelve? And what the heck, I've known Raine since we were three. He said he didn't think Lees did it, but I don't believe him. He looks guilty. It's sad*

what drugs'll make you do. Arrrggghh! People! That's what's wrong with the world! I just lit a cigarette. You should have one too. That way we'll both be smoking and writing and reading this. I like that image. Are you smoking? Are you listening to my mix-tape? Isn't it cool? I made a copy of it before I sent it and I played it for Lynnae and she loves it. She asked me to make her a copy. I am quite the DJ, if I do say so myself. As you probably noticed, I included Honey-addressed stamped envelopes. Now you don't have any excuses not to write. I'm wondering if these letters are getting to you at all. Your dad says it's the right address, but that he hasn't heard from you either. You should call him. He misses you too. Not like me though. I miss you the most. You should call me. Rochester is boring without you. All I do is go to work and come home. Last night my parents had a dinner party with two of the detectives my dad works with and their wives. They made me eat with them. My mom worked on the menu all day, but the roast was burned, the salad was over dressed in rancid olive oil, and the potatoes were raw. She didn't realize that you have to cook potatoes. We were all like, WOW, really? No one could eat any of it. Dad started teasing her, saying he was going to order pizza. Mom broke down in front of everyone. She stabbed her potato and broke her plate, then flung the potato at my dad. It hit him (thump) right in the forehead. They started this huge food fight. I got a bunch of shit in my hair. And they made me clean it up! Sometimes I wonder what I'm still doing here. My parents are like little kids. I wish they'd grow up. Tomorrow, I'm off grounding and I'm going to go see James. He called me the other day and asked why I hadn't been over. I told him it was because I was grounded because Lees stole my mom's necklace, but he didn't believe me. He asked if I'd talked with you. I told him I hadn't. That no one had. He said, "Good." He says it means you are never coming back. He said that when he gets out, he's going to "disappear completely." Who could blame him? He hasn't ever had it good. Just between you and me, I don't think he's tried hard enough. Like you. Look at you! You're a big bad-a$$ writer! You're going to be famous someday! Maybe you could write a story about us. That would be fun, to read something about yourself. Then again, maybe that wouldn't be cool. What would you say about me? About us? Oh boy, I hope I'm not giving you any ideas. Maybe you could write about someone like me. Only a little better. Make me a better person, Henry. If you ever do write about us, you know. Anyway. I hope you're getting these letters because the other two haven't come back and if you aren't getting them, then who is? If you're reading this and your name is not Henry, stop reading other *peoples' mail. Thanks.*

157 ... I re-lit and smoked the rest of my cigarette. Honey had drawn stick figure themes on several of the envelopes. I set the automatic play button on the tape player. Honey's mix was on a loop: Black Sheep, Primus, Dead Milkmen, Twisted Sister, Beastie Boys, LL Cool J. Honey was such a good girl. James was a lucky guy, to have such a dedicated lover. It was heartbreaking to think of them together, to let her go. I was going to miss her, but I promised James I'd stay away in exchange for his silence. He'd give me legal immunity in exchange for some heartache. His suffering for mine. I was honor-bound to respect our agreement.

158 ... *H,   I wish you were here. It's beautiful outside. There is a breeze coming through my window. My parents are not talking to each other today so I've been hanging out in my room. I don't know why they're even together anymore. I can't help wonder if they wouldn't be better off living alone. I'm glad you and me don't have their problems. Then again you're not writing back. You're not mad at me about something are you? If you are reading these and not writing me back it kinda makes you a hoser. You're not a hoser are you? Do you miss home yet? Home misses you. I called your house today. Your dad hasn't heard from you either. He says, No news is good news. Is it? I stayed home from work today. I'm not feeling so good. I think my period's coming. Grrrr, it really sucks that you're not here. It's been some of the best weather we've had all summer and I don't have anyone to hang around with. I guess it's not summer anymore though is it? It's September. You're in school. In Iowa. It sounds so flipping weird. Maybe I should go back to school. I'm bored just going*

to work every day. I don't want to grow up. Lynnae says I have to. We got into an argument the other day. I know you probably don't want to hear about it, but James was able to get conjugal visits and I went to meet with him. I guess I was just curious what a conjugal visit would be like. It feels a little creepy, if you ask me, like someone's going to walk in on you. Like that time I went down on you in the cemetery and the group tour walked by the car? That was embarrassing. Anyway, it was that day, but I didn't really want to do it. James got mad, he hit me. Lynnae said I shouldn't ever go back to see him again. I told her she was being dramatic. Lynnae said I don't listen to anyone, that no one likes me anymore. Do you like me Henry? You do, don't you? So why do I feel like you forgot about me? I regret not telling you that I wanted you to stay. I know you're doing what you should be doing and maybe that's why I wanted you to make love to me that night at the bridge. I want so badly to feel you inside me now. Beside me. I can feel you, you're here now with me, in my bed. We're watching the curtains move. It's going to rain I think. I just lit that incense you won me at the Christ the King Fair, the night you and James got into that fight with those guys from Irondequoit. What was that all about anyway? Will he ever change? I see you, doing so well, doing what you want, living freely. I can't help but want to be with you. I know you'll be successful, Henry. But what is success without love? Do you love me Henry? I love you.

159 … I looked out the window. The fan blades were spinning slowly. I re-read the last few lines of Honey's fourth letter. I felt guilty. I wanted to be with her. I wanted to be away from her. I'd been playing on both teams. If I went for Honey, it would only be a matter of time before James ratted me out. Of course, he knew I would do what I was told. In a sense, I was still on his side. I looked at the stack of Honey's letters. I couldn't help but continue. The next letter was short. Very short.

160 … *H,   I saw James today. It's over. He thinks it's because of you. I told him I just can't take his shit anymore. I can't stand this silence. I need you to get in touch with me. Please.*

161 … I used the phone card Dad gave me and my assigned phone code to call Honey's house. Jack answered. They still hadn't heard anything from Honey. An aunt was over. They were preparing to canvas the neighborhood. "Call your father," Jack said. It was a sincere reminder that I was still someone's child. I tried to slip into that role. I called home. Dad picked up. He sighed when he heard my voice. He asked how I was, how things were going, why I hadn't called, if I was in Iowa. I asked him where else I would be. "I don't know, Henry. Honey told me some things … I had no idea … your involvement with … her and James." I wasn't in a confessing mood. I was scared. What the hell had happened? I made excuses. I told him about my class load and the job at the Bagel Shop and moving rooms. "At least you're settled now," he said. "When did you talk to Honey?" I asked. He said, Honey had come to the house that morning. I was relieved. He said, "I promised Honey I wouldn't call her parents. But *you* can tell them. She said she's going to *California*?" I was stunned. "California?" Dad said, "I asked her to stay, to talk with me. But she said she was there just to thank me. I hate to say this Tip, she wasn't making much sense. It made me nervous."

162 ... I prayed Honey was safe somewhere. No one heard the prayer, I'm sure. We're all alone in this beauty, together.

163 ... The next letter was a doozy.

H,   The police charged James with over 50 robberies today. They moved him to a different part of the jail. They won't let me see him. They wouldn't let me talk to him in the courtroom. Do you even care? I can only wait so long – Honey

164 ... There was one more envelope. I opened it without thinking. The letter tore with it.

H,   You haven't called. You .... haven't written. I need answers. I need to get out of here .... I can't stand my own skin. I feel disgusting. Remember how we .... used to say we'd be friends to the end? Looks like you broke .... that promise. I hope you get this. I loved you Henry. I really did .... HR

165 ... I wasn't sure what to make of it. Honey had a flare for the dramatic, like her mother, but she had a level head about her, these days. That wasn't always the case. Honey attempted suicide when she was sixteen. She filled the bath tub with warm water and ate a bunch of sleeping pills.

Lucky for Honey, her sister Jackie came home unexpectedly from college for the weekend. Honey had her stomach pumped, but she was alive. When I saw her in the hospital, she said, "It was stupid. I just wanted someone to notice me." Honey's disappearance was a potentially dangerous turn. I felt like someone had catapulted the thing I wanted most toward the horizon. There was a good chance I might never find her. I imagined Honey on a comfortable trajectory through the air. The air was in her hair. She was smiling. It was an inspirational moment. I sat up and flipped through the phone book. I paged through the airlines but Honey hated to fly. I called Greyhound Bus Lines. They don't track the names of ticket holders. I hung up and tried Amtrak. The operator was promoting a new *Fall Foliage* package. "Sheila," I said. "I'm trying to find someone."

166 ... I walked toward downtown with my notebook and a pocket full of quarters. I had my instincts, but there was no telling what Honey would do. All any of us could do was wait. The ball was in her court now. She was driving this train. I stopped in front of The Airliner. There was a silhouette of a lonely bar stool inside. It was $1 beer night. I went in and sat down. The bartender placed a napkin in front of me. I showed him my fake ID and he handed it back to me. "What can I get you?" I lit a cigarette and said, "Two beers and a shot of Tequila." The bartender asked what the occasion was. "Time travel," I said.

167 ... The Airliner was slammed. I pushed the empty shot glass away and swallowed some beer. My slice of pizza arrived. I could feel my notebook in my back pocket. I had been waiting for something magnificent to come. Some new and innovative way to say the same old shit. I didn't want to

force it, but I hadn't written much since I arrived in Iowa. I had blackouts and blank pages. I was too busy, too stoned, too soft. A *writer* says *fuck it* and gets to work. I was feeling down on myself. The bartender asked if I wanted another beer with a gesture. "Keep 'em coming." I was hungry, but I wasn't going to eat until I wrote something. Not a fucking bite. I opened the notebook. The beer came. I waited. I listened. The muse wasn't talking. Jaja used to say, *Always start with a simple fact. Something that only you know.* But what did I know? Had I really climbed out of the muck of birth and the bright white light of youth to wind up on a bar stool in Iowa? It didn't seem right to squander this chance fantasy, but the years, so far, were stardust. I doubted I could trust anything I remembered. I looked around The Airliner, at the insecure faces, the macho men, the professors and grad students, the bodies treading bodies. *This* was my own failed destiny. There was a single blank page across from a game of hangman in the back of the notebook. The stick figure had been killed, but Honey hadn't completed the phrase. _ove an_ ma_hem.

168 ... I sucked down the last of my beer and stared at the blank page. My pizza was cold. The cheese and grease congealed. It didn't look good anymore. It looked sad. Uneaten food always does. There was a hubbub in the corner, some kind of hoopla. Several people were hollering and pointing. Someone was crawling on the floor through the crowd. It was G. G saw me too. He stopped as the bouncer made his way through the crowd. "Hash!" G said, standing up. His hair was all fucked up, long on one side and short on the other. I didn't get a chance to ask why he was on the floor or what happened to his hair because the bouncer was picking him up by the suspenders. He hauled G through the crowd like a sack of bread. Someone opened the door. It was a good thing they did, I think the bouncer would have used G's head to open it. G was wiggling, shouting, screaming, laughing. None of it was very clear. Someone in the crowd looked at the person next to them. "Did he say the water's poisoned?" It was what I thought he said too. They both looked at their drinks and set them on

the bar beside me. G was pacing back and forth in front of the bar, chanting something at the bouncer. It was like watching the cartoon Tasmanian Devil in slow motion.

169 ... Currier Hall was quiet. The hallways were too. It was a welcome uncertainty, the lack of something happening. There was a low-grade buzz coming from each room, a focusing on what mattered – homework, friendship, love. It wasn't a sensation that I was ready to tap into. I had something else on my mind. Someone was on the floor, in front of N333. It was Honey. There was an irrevocable chill that crashed over me. I could almost feel James' cold hard grip on my neck. I couldn't breathe. I couldn't stop him now. He was going to do what he was going to do. Honey's hair was draped over her face and the backpack she was using as a pillow. I knelt down. Her breathing was shallow. Her hands were under her cheek like she was praying. She opened her eyes slowly and whispered, "Yay, I found you! Wow, I was having a dream." I asked her what the dream was about. Honey said, "We climbed a tree. There was a storm or something. The limb we were on broke." I asked her what happened. She smiled, "I don't know, you woke me up." We paused there, for a second and just enjoyed the other's company. I asked Honey what she was doing in Iowa. She said, "It's a lot different than I thought. Can we go inside? This floor is disgusting."

170 ... Unlocking the door to N333 I told Honey, "I *just* got all your letters. You had me worried." Honey followed me in, looking around, unimpressed. "I'm sorry about that. I was hoping those got lost. This is where you're living now?" She sat down and bounced on my bed. "Very 1990s

bachelor. Are you going to grow a goatee too?" She opened her backpack. "Can I smoke?" I turned on the fan and offered her an ash tray. She said, "You're staring." I told her I was surprised to see her. "*Happy* to see me?" she asked. I nodded, "Very." I wanted to move but the cold plaster wall was calming. I said, "Does James know you're here?" Honey scoffed. "Don't worry about James. He's not going to be getting out any time soon." In jail or out, a deal was a deal. Honey didn't know about the arrangement James and I had. She didn't know that I promised not to come back, not to pursue her in any way. Honey looked out the window and smoked. She said, "You have a nice view." I pulled myself away from the wall. "I like mine better."

171 ... It's my nature. I seduced Honey until we were lying down on my rickety twin bed. She said, "Give me your hand. I missed you." I told her I missed her too. She said, "Have you met a lot of people here?" I told her what I knew about the university and about temporary housing and my classes. "I was asking if you've slept with anyone," she said. I told her that there was "someone" I had "gotten to know." She looked at me as if I made some ridiculous and lewd comment. She said, "I thought so." I asked her what she meant by that. Honey said, "I know you, H ... What's her name? Did you use protection?" I told Honey she was being "retarded. Is that why you came here? To check up on me?" It was like I insulted her. "I came, because you asked me to come, H."

172 ... It was the kindest form of torture, watching Honey undress from across the room, and wrap herself in a towel. "Get it out of your head, H. I need a shower. I'm disgusting. All this, down here, it's a cesspool. Which

way to the shower?" I gestured in the direction of the showers and Honey left. I was confused. There were flashes of sentimental moments where I might have said something to give Honey the impression that I wanted her to follow me to Iowa, but I don't and I didn't remember that. I don't remember ever, blatantly, instigating it. Then again, I can't understand why I would flee. James was in jail. Honey and I had all the time in the world to do what we wanted. She was my best friend, my confidant, the most beautiful woman I had ever been with. Living without her was the hardest thing to take. It was something worth noting – the one time Tantalus actually reached the water, tricked the fruit tree, and dodged the falling boulder. It deserved a poem. I was writing it when Honey came back. "That was soooo necessary. What are you doing?" she said. I tapped the notebook with the tip of my pen, "Writing something." It was the first time in weeks that anything had come easy. The handwriting was sloppy, but something is better than nothing. Honey snatched the notebook from me. She read it to herself, then said, "What's wrong with friendship, H?" She handed me the notebook, wiped something from my face with the moist towel and kissed me. The towel fell to the floor. She knelt down on it and pushed me back. The rest, I'll keep for myself.

173 … I looked out the window while Honey got dressed. Two guys were playing basketball on the court behind Burge Hall. "I can't believe you don't have a brush!" Honey said. She was wearing jeans and a tight blue t-shirt with white lettering: EXPLORE YOUR FUTURE. "Dressed to kill," I said. Honey posed for a moment and said, "It's the nicest stuff I brought." I asked her if she wanted to call her parents. She used her fingers to comb her hair and said, "I don't want to talk to them. They're going to yell at me, then I'm going to yell at them. That'll bum everyone out. I just want to spend tonight with you. We can worry about everyone else tomorrow. What's there to do in this town?"

174 … I reached for Honey's hand as we walked. Each time I connected she pulled away. "Where are you taking me?" she asked. I stopped. We were there. I gestured to the Delta house. "A frat? Really H, you *have* changed," Honey said. "I know a guy that lives here. He's usually holding." That was all I needed to say. Honey was a head like I was a head. I led her inside and upstairs to the Gymnasium. I knocked. Rugby opened the door and smiled. "I knew Hash would be back!" Rugby hugged me and I introduced Honey and asked if he had anything good. The three of us sat down on the couch under the loft bed. There was a new fish tank on the bookshelf. Honey leaned on the back of the couch and said, "I love clown fish!" Rugby asked if Honey was cool. I vouched for her and Rugby handed me a round piece of glass with a mound of coke in the center. There was a razor and a tiny shovel. I felt like God for a moment, reversing an avalanche to ward off my boredom. When I was done, Honey took a sizable bump and said, *"Heh-llo!"* The door opened. "Hello!" Paul said, leading Karen into the Gymnasium. Paul locked the door. Everyone noticed Karen and Honey's resemblance. Karen looked at Honey, Karen looked at me. Honey looked at me. Honey knew it was Karen who I'd been *exploring*. "Looks like we're just in time," Karen said. Paul squatted by the table, drew out five lines on the glass and loaded up. He handed the coke to Karen. Karen folded three lines into one and sucked the whole thing up one side of her face. Then, emotionless as a rope, she asked, "Who's your friend Hash?" Honey gave me a look. *"Hash?"* I introduced Honey to Karen and Paul. *"Honey,"* Karen said. "Isn't that sweet?"

175 … Karen was looking at Honey like she wanted to fuck her. The sounds coming from downstairs were large, growing more random. All I wanted to do was get in, get high, and get out of there. Before I could make a move, Karen took Honey's hand and said, "Let's let the boys be

boys for a while." Honey didn't know what to make of Karen's gesture. I didn't feel comfortable letting Honey go anywhere with Karen alone. I offered to go with them. "She's a big girl," Karen said. "I can take care of myself," Honey added.

176 ... Some time later I found Honey outside in the shadows beside the house. She looked at me like a helium balloon with a face drawn on it. She laughed and pointed at me and hissed. "What do you know?" I said. "Depends," Karen answered, stepping from the half-light. I didn't want or need her chaos. I wanted a drastic sensory mutation that would erase it all so I could start over again, be some one I could believe in. Karen showed me a small metal canister. Inside were colorful paper squares. I looked at Honey. She had an enormous smile on her face. She said, "I'm Miss Cotton Candy." Karen turned the lid over. There was a paste smeared inside the lid. She said, "The blotters will get you there, but I know you've been *there* before. This is *wash*. Someone I know laid a ten-lot of the *White Fluff* blotter. The *wash* is the residue from the pan the paper was in." Honey came close and pointed at the *wash* and said, "All you have to do is touch it. That's all. Then wham!" Honey looked sharply at me and pulled me close. Her eyes were diluted murder. "Let's play," she said.

177 ... The *wash* was like being in an accident ... in slow motion. By the time I realized how powerful it might be it was way too late to turn back, to avoid it, to prepare for it. Getting from Delta to Currier Hall was like walking through a wax museum in strobe light. Honey and I tumbled into N333. We were safe. We took turns looking through the security port. The view only made our paranoia more telescopic. We were enchanted by the

point of view. "Oh," Honey said, pulling herself away. "The mix tape! Put it on, put it on!" All I had to do was push play on the radio. Honey fidgeted. She was looking for anything to keep her racing mind from the seriousness of our climb. "This stuff is really powerful," she said. It was rare for either of us to feel this way – to be out of control. We had navigated prolonged acid trips and come back from the wilderness unscathed, but the *wash* was causing blackouts punctuated by carnivalic flashes. We were trapped in a wormhole of pauses … The next thing I knew, Honey was in a tangle of Christmas lights, spinning on her back, singing, then getting up to rewind a song to play it again. I was entirely in my own head, building secret realities and mumbling about the choices. Honey was upside down against the wall. The Christmas lights were all around her. Something fell out of her pocket. It was a small vile of coke. She smiled and said, "I might have taken a little" from Rugby and Paul. It was the trigger that shot us into hyperspace.

178 … We each took a couple of bumps and I got an erection. I couldn't help it. Honey watched as my thing rose. It was a curiosity to the both of us. When it seemed to have reached maximum capacity, Honey poked it and it grew some more. She said, "Does that mean you want to have sex?" The thought of penetrating her was gross. I could hear the sounds, like the tearing of a pit from a peach, our sweaty bodies heaving, colliding. I covered my face with my hands. "*No*." Between my fingers, I saw the spray can of furniture polish. It was an impulsive moment. I had an idea and a burst of energy. I flipped the bed frame on its side and positioned the mattress like a backstop against the wall opposite the door. I sprayed the wax on the floor and used a T-shirt to polish the tiles. I went to the far end of the room and ran toward the mattress, sliding across the floor like a puck until I crashed into the soft backstop. Honey was giggling into her hands. The mix-tape was playing a song we liked. Honey stopped laughing. She stared off into a short deep distance and said, "How can you even move right now? My legs are in my ears."

179 … "Wow," Honey said, laughing into a deep sigh that helped her to focus. "I didn't know you could break-dance." I remembered enough of the routine from fifth grade to improvise. I'm sure the way the *wash* was manipulating Honey's reality, I probably looked like a clumsy genius. The room was a disaster. During my attempt at a backspin, I knocked the lamp off the desk. When I tried to perform a dolphin, I kicked the chair over. A seam in the tiles pulled out a clump of my hair when I went for a head-spin, but Honey seemed impressed nonetheless. When I ran out of dance moves, Honey said, "I'm feeling a little claustrophobic." We donned sunglasses and stuffed our pockets with things we thought we would need. Then Honey and I left N333. We ran down the North stairway and out into the night, down the walkway toward the river. We weren't speaking. We were rushing into a new, much wilder reality. The sounds of crickets and trees and water blended with the electric buzz of the university. When we got to the river walk, Honey found a rock in the grass and drew a hop-scotch board on the sidewalk. One of the nicest things about being with Honey was how playful she could be. As unknown and serious as so many things are in life, when I was with Honey I enjoyed being alive. We both took a deep breath. We were past the worst of it. Honey threw the rock and hopped through the squares and said, "Iowa is beautiful *H* … Or … Do you want me to call you *Hash* now?" I didn't have any answers. The west side of campus was doused in an orange glow under a pale midnight sky and I was caught up in it.

180 … Honey and I walked along the river to the train bridge near the EPB. "You and your trains," she said. "What's the attraction?" I tried to explain a train's iconic freedom and power, their ability and weight but

some things are difficult to describe when you're tripping. We walked out on the rails and dangled our feet over the water. Honey said, "I just don't get it, going to the *Can of Worms* the way you do..." I corrected her, "The way I did." Honey repeated me. "Right. You don't live in Rochester any more." I changed the subject. I said, "My Dad told me about California." Honey didn't understand. "California?" I told her what Dad said about her visit, "Was that yesterday, morning?" Honey and I were amazed by the amount of time and the quantity of living which had occurred between the previous morning and that moment. She said, "Wow, that was yesterday. But I was only quoting Led Zeppelin. You know, *Going to California with an aching in my heart*. He really thought I was going to California?" We laughed off the absurdity of language and understanding and I asked Honey what her immediate plans were. She said, "*That* is a good question. I hope it includes a bathroom. Is there somewhere we could ... quick?" The EPB was open. We found the restrooms and relieved ourselves in different stalls simultaneously. I farted as a joke. Honey said, "Are you done? Get out. Please?" While Honey finished up, I found the vending area and grooved us some snacks. I heard her calling me from down the hall and whistled until she found me. I showed her what I had scored and asked if she wanted me to groove anything else. She said, "I can't eat right now. I've got cramps. Let's go back outside. This building is freezing."

181 ... We opened our *Chocodiles* on the steps of the Old Capital, overlooking the communications building, the EPB, the train bridge, and the River Walk. "I can't believe you've never had one of these," I said. I broke mine in half and showed her. "It's a chocolate-covered Twinkie." Honey bit into her *Chocodile*. She read the wrapper and mumbled while chewing, "Someone should probably be put away for this. The shelf life on these things is criminal. Mmm. That is good." There were reams of questions flooding the moments we were not speaking. I was desperately in-love, infatuated, confused, stupefied. Honey was with me. She was safe. For the first time in a long time it didn't matter what James was doing, planning, or thinking. I had won the prize that he had been struggling for so long to

control. What's better, Honey had come to me of her own free will. She finished the *Chocodile* and crumpled the wrapper. It was a beautiful night, the perfect setting. Honey threw her wrapper at me and said, "Stop staring at me *weirdo*! Do you mind if we go back?" The way she said it, I thought that something was wrong. "It's girl stuff," she said.

182 ... I opened the door to N333. The Christmas lights were still on. The tape player was squealing. The tape had ended, but the automatic stop hadn't engaged. Honey pressed STOP. I shut the door, turned the bed over, and turned on the fan. "Do you want anything? Water? Another Chocodile?" Honey groaned, moving to the bed. "No, thank you. Come here," she said, laying down. "Put your fingers here." She pulled her shirt up. She unzipped her pants and opened the flaps. I said something crass. "Just press," she said. I pressed. She bit her lip. "Not so hard." I lightened up. Touching her was like spinning around under a starry night, the euphoria was nauseating. I had to tame it. In that moment, I knew, or at least I thought I understood why I appealed to her. Why she might choose me over James. I had a softer side. I wanted to do something with my life. I had potential, a future. She moved my hand and winced. "Right there," she said. The weight of my hand seemed to suffice. But was it enough? "Honey," I said. Honey stopped me. She looked me square in the eye. "You don't have to analyze this, *H*. It is what it is. I know you want to understand. But, we aren't what we were yesterday and we aren't what we're going to be tomorrow. We're only right now. Sometimes," she paused. "I wish you'd stop trying to define everything all the time. I want your attention. You can give me that, can't you?" She continued to press my fingers into her belly. I said. "I always have."

183 ... The *wash* receded. The sun was coming up. A sliver of light found its way through the curtain and fan blades to the bed. We laid down and Honey rolled onto her right side. I spooned in behind her. Honey said, "I didn't mean to scare you with the letters. I thought you were ignoring me." Her hair fell alongside her face. I wanted her to know that she could trust me. I said, "I wasn't ignoring you. *And* ... you can stay with me as long as you want. I have a cafeteria card for food, and I have classes, but you can do whatever you want, in your own time, on your own terms. I just want to move forward." What I meant in that moment is that I wanted to write. I wanted to find a little privacy. I wanted a day without interruption and a story to tell. Now that I have the words and all the time in the world, all I want is Honey. She was drawing circles on my arm. Her hands were soft and cold. She asked for a blanket. I got my wool blanket out of a box and covered her. We went to sleep holding each other. It was pretty boring stuff, just laying there, but my heart was pounding. For the first time in a long time, I was confident. It wasn't the drugs. It was the girl.

184 ... I was sleeping. Honey rolled over and groaned. She wrapped her arms around me. She was shivering, cold to the touch. I asked her if she was okay. She said, "I think my period's coming. Ugh, I don't have any pads." I told Honey I had seen some in the vending machines down-stairs. It wouldn't take me long. Honey said, "That's sweet H. I would love something chocolaty to eat though." I went to the sink and washed my face. My pupils were the black center of the sun. The *wash* was tak-ing another lap through my system, energizing my intentions, sending me on another adventure. I made my way to the vending area, fingering the groover in my pocket. The vending machines were freshly stocked. The selection was mind-boggling. I grooved a chocolate bar and a couple of sodas. There were sanitary pads in another machine. I used the change that I got from the sodas and chocolate to pay for the pads. When I bent down to retrieve them from the reachway, I saw a pair of shiny black shoes, a pair of creased grey pants, and the rest of a university cop. "That time of

the month?" he asked. I was embarrassed, but he didn't give me time to live out the shame. He said, "I'm concerned about something." He reached into his pocket and put some coins into one of the machines I grooved. "If I put my money in here, is it going to work?" He was brawny. He had a mustache. "It worked for me," I said walking away. "Eh, eh, eh. I didn't say you could go. Why don't you show me that thing you have in your pocket?"

185 ... He walked behind me, trying to chat me up. Cops are always so friendly when they have you in custody. They want you to feel comfortable, like they understand who you are. After all, your problem is their problem. It's an investigative tactic. They want you to incriminate yourself. It makes their job easier. But this guy was a university cop. He was in it for the illusion of power. "Stop," he said and opened a door. The room was small and warm and it smelled. "Sit down," he said. There was a chair, a desk and a set of monitors showing the main foyer, the front of the dorm and all of the main hallways on the ground floor. There was a camera trained on the vending area. He sat behind the flimsy metal desk and said, "You look familiar." I told him I have one of those faces and pointed at the television screens. "Isn't that an invasion of privacy?" He turned and looked at the closed circuit monitors. "The school has to protect its investments." I knew he meant the vending machines, but I wanted to be a dick. "You mean the students, right?" He took his time writing up a ticket, asking me for all the numbers and things that track us. I asked if he needed my shoe size. "No," he said. I was in a mood I guess. "Do you ever feel like you're wasting you're time here, Officer..." I pointed at a nameplate, "Dunn?" He didn't look up from his task. He said, "It's my job. I don't have to justify it. Especially to you." He handed me the ticket and said, "Read it. Is all the information correct?" I looked at the ticket. He described my groover as a *trick-dollar bill*. The rest of the words were blurry. Focus is a problem on the downside of a binge. "I know you have to keep the stuff I grooved, but can I take the MaxiPads? They're not for me." There was a brief argument about my paying for the pads with stolen

money. Finally, he just ended it. "You're making this more painful than it has to be."

186 ... The sun was coming up. N333 was dark and quiet. A draft of air caught the door and slammed it shut. I undressed and crawled into bed. Honey was still and silent, peaceful, hot, unresponsive. I rolled her over. "Honey?" I leapt off the bed and turned the light on. Her face was gaunt, grainy, gray, green. Her eyes were blank. She was making a fish face and she was shaking. I knelt down beside her and called her name, screamed it. I spanked her cheek. I shook her. I was terrified. I picked up the telephone. The operator answered, "Nine-one-one, what's your emergency?"

187 ... Paramedics and campus security were on their way. The operator wanted me to stay on the line, but I had to get rid of the dope. She was asking a lot of questions. I was speaking in panic tones, stuffing my mouth with marijuana, talking with my mouth full. "Could you repeat your name please, sir? Did you say Henrietta?" I covered the mouthpiece and snorted a pile of coke and rubbed some in my mouth to numb the cuts from mari-juana stems. The operator asked if Honey had taken any drugs or alcohol. She asked me if I saw any pills? I didn't have time to respond. There was a knock at the door. Honey wasn't shaking anymore. She was still, stiff. I put the phone down and tried to open the door, but the lock was stuck. I got frustrated. They were pounding on the door and Honey looked dead. I was pounding and shouting and trying to make things better, but every-thing I seemed to be doing was backfiring. Honey looked like a corpse. I was so scared that my hand began to twitch. My arm went numb. It was euphoric, the worst time in the world for a seizure.

188 … We all eventually return to the anonymous dimension. The seizures lead me close. The breath brings me back. Question is, will any of this matter in a context that is not my own?

189 … I was sure. There were angels among us. Their wings were waving in silhouette. I couldn't make anything out of it. My stomach punched. The sound was ferocious. What I had eaten wanted out. I was sitting on the floor in the hall, across from N333. The paramedics lifted Honey onto a gurney and quickly rolled her into the hall. I had the feeling she looked better, but Officer Dunn had a hold on my arm. A paramedic was shining a flashlight into my eyes. All I heard were pieces: *Happened? What did you take?* I was in "Hand-cuffs?" Language was an accessory. "Answer the question," Dunn said. "I get seizures," I said. Dunn's lips were two fish. They were flailing, splashing halotosic spittle onto the hairs of his mustache. "Two times in one hour. That can't be a coincidence," Dunn said. The paramedic asked Dunn to take off *the bracelets*? If Dunn hadn't stopped me downstairs when he did, I might have been with Honey when she went under. I might have been able to do something to help her sooner. I told Dunn, "This is your fault." He laughed. "What did I do?"

190 … Raine called while I was writing. Jack and Jean were going somewhere. They were packing the car. I thanked him and got ready to get
over there. My heart was racing. It's been a while since I've broken into
anyone's house with the explicit intention of stealing, let alone a cop's
home. I was relieved, actually, when Raine called right back. He said,
"False alarm. Jack just called. They aren't going anywhere. They're taking
Honey's stuff to Goodwill. He needs a hand carrying a dresser down the
stairs. Is there anything I should look for, or try to save?" I didn't know
what *wouldn't* be worth saving.

191 … I let the paramedic lead me to a small white ambulance with yellow lights on top. Officer Dunn was helping. The paramedic told him to
"take it easy." A crowd had gathered outside Currier Hall. People were
looking out their windows. Cars were slowing in the street. Honey's
ambulance had left. Dunn took the handcuffs off and held a bottle of my
medicine. He shook the pills and said, "Listen kid, none of this is giving
me a warm feeling. What's Etho-sux-i-mide?" The paramedic answered
for me, "It's an anticonvulsant. Have you taken any today, Henry?" I
shook my head *No*. The paramedic took the pills from Dunn and asked me
to lie down. He placed an oxygen mask over my face and read the label
on the Rx bottle. Dunn wanted to keep me there, to pursue the crimes he
thought I committed. The paramedic told Dunn to stand back. I managed
to give Dunn the finger as the doors closed. The paramedic told the driver
we were clear. He began filling out a form and asked, "Is there anyone you
want us to call?"

192 … The doctor on call said they weren't releasing me, "yet." Honey

was in another part of the hospital. That's all anyone would tell me. They gave me a temporary room, something small with a window overlooking the courtyard. There was a pool of light in the sky and clouds on the horizon. We would have some weather. I paced until things became clearer. The evening's adventures rewound and replayed, stopping and starting on a single evil flash in Karen's eye.

193 … I was faint, but I had to find Honey. I had a wheelchair. I rolled myself into the hall and started for the Emergency Room. The hospital was new, from the floor tiles to the message boards on the walls. I followed the signs and slipped past the nurses and doctors and Emergency Registration, through a large set of doors to where the patients were. Several rooms separated by curtains offered glimpses into other people's misery. I passed Honey and didn't realize it. She called to me from inside an oxygen mask. She was weak, sedated, on pain killers. I rolled up to the side of her bed. She was hooked up to an IV, the only patient in a two-bed "room." The sheets were pulled down to her lap and she was smiling, steaming up the inside of her mask. She tapped the IV drip chamber. "Good stuff," she said. "Why are you in a wheelchair? What are you wearing?" I put the breaks on and stood up, modeling the gown. I told Honey about the seizure and asked if they knew what was wrong with her. Honey didn't know. She said, "They took a lot of blood. I'm waiting for an ultrasound." I took her hand. She looked at my wrists and remembered something. "Were you in handcuffs?"

194 … Honey used me to get to James before. I knew it. She knew it. James knew it. But, James had also used me to get to her. It was a pattern

I was used to. My parents used me to pass messages to one another for years. No matter how I delivered the message, without their body language and presence of delivery, I'm afraid all I was offering anyone were the words. I put my hand on Honey's arm. The machines around her hissed and beeped. "There's something I need to tell you, Hon." She crinkled her brow. She was in LaLaland. I wanted to tell her everything, every secret detail, each emotional firework that led me to set James up. I wanted to tell her that I did it so I could be with her. I took a breath and said, "I, uh ... I set James up ... I'm the reason he's in jail ...." I went over the details of the night James was arrested, how I cased the house and removed the home security sign. "I wanted to be with you. I did it so we could be together." Honey interrupted me. She said, "You were with me that night." I repeated myself. I didn't understand what she was telling me. She pulled the oxygen mask off. "You are the good guy in this story, H. You were with me that night. Whatever James did, whenever James did it. You were with me." I understood what she was telling me, but I didn't believe it. Why was Honey throwing herself in traffic for me? "There's something you *don't* know," Honey added. "James came over one night. He was covered in blood, totally panicking. He was insane. I think he killed someone." Had James finally gone too far? Had he really taken someone's life? There was no time for more questions. Something was wrong. Honey's monitors and machines went berserk. The nurses ran to her bedside and asked what happened. I told them we were talking. "She just ... went blank."

195 ... When the panic subsided, I realized I was telling my life story to a kid. He was sitting beside me in a fiberglass chair in the hall outside Honey's new room. I told some lady I'd watch the kid while she went to the bathroom. He was eating caramel popcorn from a box, uninterested in my rambling. He handed me one of the malformed kernels with a nut attached. I ate it and kept talking. The kid said I shouldn't chew and talk at the same time. "You could choke." I chewed the rest of it and said, "At least she's stable. One of the nurses tried to get me to go back to my room. I told her

to suck on it. The hell I'm going anywhere." I extended my hand to the kid for some more caramel popcorn as the lady came back. He gave the lady a big smile and said, "Hey mom. Suck on it." She wasn't pleased. She asked him where he learned that phrase. He looked at me. We were both in trouble. "Kids," I laughed. "They say the funniest things sometimes."

196 … Honey was in a daze. The drugs held her in stasis. She would sleep for a while and then reanimate. Simple conversations were spread over minutes. Others remained uncompleted. I held her hand and waited. It gave me a purpose. I was terribly happy and confused and angry. My dream had arrived, but it was damaged. One way or another I was determined to love her from our dented pasts forward. I gripped Honey's hand for my own affirmation. She woke up. She was aware. She had this Mona Lisa kind of smile. She said, "Oooh, yum. I was dreaming about Gummy bears and non-pareils." I asked her if she wanted me to get her some candy. She tapped my hand and said, "No, no. You're very … sweet Henry … You know, it's taken a lot for me … to understand your love." I didn't completely understand what she was going through or getting at, so I responded with what my gut was telling me to say. "I always wondered where love could lead us. Now, I'm wondering why we weren't trying to lead love." Honey said, "You flatter me." I told her, "You *complement* me." I was in love. I think maybe Honey was too. I was going to try for it. Even if the magnetism of our proximity was repelling us. Our future was a landscape that could span lifetimes in any direction and still barely scratch the surface of Eternity. God was watching us walk through His garden. Honey took a short breath and tried to move a little. She winced from a pain I still did not understand. The pain seemed to subside, but I was already day-dreaming again. Holding Honey's hand somehow connected me to the universe. I knew the meaning of life. It was very simple. Enjoy *this*. Delight in the moments you have, because you never know when it might be over. It sounds fatalistic, simplistic, and lame, I know. But if the impending moment of death brings life into perspective, then I think that's a good thing. If I could maintain *that* sensation I had in *that* moment, I

might be filled with some contentment now. Unfortunately, that's not how this works. "Marry me," I said. Honey laughed and said, "You're crazy!" I was ten steps ahead of her, scattering rose petals in the church aisle. Just then, as strange as it is to write it, there was a flare of light outside. A second flare confirmed it. "Fireworks!" They were going off every couple of seconds. Honey tried to sit up. She liked the fizzlers. I liked the big ones I could feel in my chest. Honey gave me a look, her eyes reflecting the colorful pyrotechnics. I said it again. "Marry me." Honey smiled and nodded, but she didn't have time to answer. She puckered her lips and exhaled forcefully. I asked her if she wanted me to call for the nurse. She nodded and said, "Something bad is happening."

197 ... A good shriek can tear the fabric of time. Honey's parents were in freak-out mode in the doorway of Honey's hospital room. Jack was cradling Jean. Jean was in a tizzy. The Riders were flanked by a dark-haired stranger. The nurses were stabilizing Honey. The heavy-set nurse led me to the door. I walked into the hall on my own steam. Jean whimpered angrily, "What did *you* do to my little girl?!" Jack wrapped his arms around Jean, more to keep her from me than to comfort her. Honey said, "Mom? Dad?" The nurses tried to stop Jack, but they could only detain him. There was little preventing him from standing at his little girl's bedside. "What are you doing here?" Honey asked weakly. Jean rushed to her bedside and took Honey's hand. Jack said, "The hospital called this morning. We got on the first bird out." I would come to learn that the awkward dark-haired stranger with the Riders was the hospital chaplain. He met the Riders on the airplane. It was serendipity. He had been at a conference in Rochester. They got to talking and the chaplain offered to help them find Honey. He was dressed in street clothes. His black shirt was tucked into his blue jeans. He was wearing running shoes, carrying a duffel bag. The chaplain extended his hand in my direction and said, "I'm Jason, by the way. You must be ... James?"

198 … Jack walked toward me while Jean stayed at Honey's bedside. I
had been listening from the door. "You really had us in a mess," Jean told
Honey. Jack is a big man. I felt small, but not intimidated. He put his hand
on my shoulder. He whispered, "Thank you for keeping us informed. Your
dad called us this morning. Moments later the hospital called. It was good
to know that she was … some where … at least." He was visibly upset
and relieved. He found his composure and turned to look at me squarely.
"Did Honey tell you why she ran away, Henry?" I said "She must have …
felt she needed … t-to get away for a w-while." I stutter when I'm nervous. Jack sighed and leaned forward. "As a parent, you wonder if you did
everything right. If there's something you could have done better." Jack
wasn't interested in my opinions of his family's dynamics. He was fishing for answers, bating his lures. I was prepared for almost any question
he could have asked. "Henry," he said. "How well do you know James?" I
felt the blood drain from my face.

199 … There are a lot of ways to deal with a cop. In this instance that cop
was my best friend's father. I tried to imagine Jack as my father-in-law,
spending my weekend afternoons barbecuing in the Riders' backyard with
him and all of his cop buddies. I answered as honestly as I could. "I have
a lot of questions myself. I doubt I will ever get answers to them. Even
the most transparent people can lead secret lives." It was a good answer,
but it was too vague for Jack. He wasn't satisfied. He said, "What's his
relationship with my daughter?" I told Jack that I believed Honey's relationship with James was over. He said, "Jail can do that. You must have
heard? James was charged with murder." As a cop, he would have known
the intimate details of any charges. If James pointed a finger at me, for any
reason, like he said he would, it would have been in my best interest to tell

my side of the story. I just wasn't taking the bait.

200 ... I looked Jack squarely in the eye. "What can I tell you? James had it tough as a kid. His dad is violent. He was in and out of foster care, juvie, jail." Jack asked how the three of us got together. For me, it was simple. "Proximity, I guess. James and I grew up together. We lived on the same street. The *three of us* rode the same bus. We had the same classes. It was ... organic." Jack asked if I knew about the risks James was taking. I said, "I *suspected* he was up to something. I just never asked." Jack leaned back and sneered. "You kids these days. No one ever asks questions. Why is that?" I understood that it was a rhetorical question, but I answered him anyway. "It's one of two things," I said. "We either don't care or we take things for granted. We're grazing creatures. When we find something we want, we consume it until it's gone and then we move on. But ... some of us are satisfied with *enough*." Jack thought about it and asked, "Which one are you?" The words came freely when I spoke about Honey. I said, "I've wondered about that myself. I think I've found something special here. It's what *I* would call *enough*." Jack chuckled and said, "Iowa, of all places."

201 ... The doctor was running. Jack and I knew something was wrong. I stayed in the doorway. Jack followed the doctor into Honey's room. Honey was holding her right abdomen. Jean was backing away. Honey and I made eye contact. She was in awe of the pain she was in. The doctor very calmly commented. "Surgery ... Time is of the essence." The nurses were moving Honey's bed before any of us were able to process the information. Everyone was tense. The nurses maneuvered Honey's bed into the hall. The doctor stayed behind to fill Jack and Jean in on what was hap-

pening. Honey managed to convince the nurses to stop. "One second. One second," Honey said. "H? H. Find the hiding place, under the carpet. Stay put. I like Iowa." I didn't understand. The cryptic message would have to suffice. The hospital had her.

202 … If I saw me on the street, I would have avoided me. In the hospital, I was an expected quality, disheveled, sickly, weak. Some people smiled at me. Others asked if I needed help getting to where I was going. I approached one of the information desks and told the nurse I was lost. She told me I wasn't too far off and pointed in the direction I needed to go. When I found the cafeteria, I wandered around looking for Jack and Jean. I heard my name being called from somewhere near the windows. Jean was standing next to a corner table where Jack was sitting. Their backs were to an open courtyard and a bus stop. I made my way toward their table, examining the piles of food on other people's plates and trays. I was hungry and weak. There were times in my life where hunger was the norm, where hunger achieved its own euphoria, it's own understanding. Jack took a bite of something and offered me a meal ticket. By the looks of what everyone was eating, it was morning. I could have sworn it was still evening. My sense of linear progress was tweaked. I guess that happens when you're malnourished, taking seizures between shots of adrenalin.

203 … I came back to the table with a glass of water and a plate of bacon. Jean was talking to herself. Jack was comforting her. I sipped the water, unsure why they wanted to see me. Jean said, "She was very quiet. A quiet child. Honey didn't cry when she was born. She just opened her eyes and yawned." I told them, "I cried a lot. I was a sick kid." I wasn't looking

for pity. I wondered if Honey ever mentioned the absences. I didn't think I'd ever had one when they were around, but I wasn't the best person to say when or where they happened. I looked at the Riders and then at my hand. It was twitching again. I put it under the table. Jack had seen it. He gave me a concerned look. I didn't want to segue into a conversation about epilepsy, but I didn't want it to be a surprise when and if I had a seizure in their presence. "I get seizures," I said. Jean nodded, and reengaged the conversation, "That's a lot of bacon."

204 ... Bacon has an ethereal effect on me. I was talking fast, burning through the countless misdiagnoses that led to *Lennox-Gastaut* syndrome and the ketogenic diet that turned me into a bacon addict. I'm sure they didn't want all the details, but when you're on a roll, sometimes you just have to go with it. Sadly, every roll comes to an end eventually. We were sitting in silence when Jean asked if I liked Iowa. I told them that I was still adjusting. "How's the writing?" Jack asked. I didn't have the heart to tell anyone that I hadn't been accepted into the Writers Workshop. I told them it looked "promising." Even I wasn't sure what I meant. We were just taking steps toward heaven. "I'm working on a novel," I said. Jack leaned back in his chair. "A novel? What's it about?" I wasn't even sure why I said it. I guess lies can fill a space as much as the truth. "Relation-ships and God," I said. Jean was a big fan of the Christian organizations around Rochester. She said, "Those are good subjects to write about." She was suddenly very interested. I felt compelled to keep lying to her. I said, "I haven't worked on it in a few weeks, with the move and all, but it's about a guy named John. His wife leaves him. For weeks he mopes around the house cataloging the whys and maybies of his marriage, the emptiness of the house, the handwriting in the Dear John letter. But, the more he thinks about it, about her, the more he drives himself into a kind of de-pressed insanity. One night, he lights the house on fire and drives off into the sunset." Jean interrupted me. "That's not about God. It's about an ar-sonist." Jack said, "Let him finish. There's probably more to it?" I assured them that there was, but I had to pause to give myself enough space to plot

it. I said, "John drives west. He sleeps in the car, eats in diners, just passes the time. One rainy night, out of loneliness, he picks up a hitchhiker." Jean didn't like it one bit. She said, "Offering rides to strangers is inviting bad luck into your life." I nodded and said, "Maybe. This time, however, the hitchhiker is God."

205 ... Jack said, "You're serious about this?" I'm sure, for the Riders, being a writer was a troublesome career path, something that inevitably led to poverty. I said, "It's *my* one chance to do something with my life." I knew and know that no one is going to do it for me. It's up to *me* to write something worth a shit. It's up to me to communicate some semblance of *Truth*. Lucky for me, I don't have to write faster or harder than anyone else. All I have to do is cut myself and bleed on the page. I knew that if I gave it enough time, I could get the bleeding right. All I needed was a moment of inspiration. All I needed was a story. I got goose bumps. I was ready for anything. "When did you find out?" Jean asked. I thought she was asking me about writing, about the moment I discovered that it would be my life's work. I said, "I must have been sixteen? I found my sister's poetry journal ...." It was obvious that we weren't on the same page. "No," Jean interrupted. "When did you find out about Honey's pregnancy?"

206 ... I was dumfounded, awestruck, sideswiped. But I knew when it happened, if it happened with me. The moment of conception. Honey and I were under the Veterans Memorial Bridge, getting high, climbing on the caged rocks. Honey had never been there. This was where I went to be alone, to write. We finished the joint we were smoking and sat down on one of the cages of rocks. Honey leaned her head on my shoulder. We

kissed. We stopped. We kissed again. One thing led to another. There was no effort, no struggle. We wanted to be there. We wanted to be with each other. I was overwhelmed by how amazing she felt. I told her as much. Honey smiled and made it feel better. The whole act was dangerously quick. I tried to pull away, but she wrapped her legs around my back as I came and the two of us continued softly fucking, kissing, smiling, breathless, satisfied, and happy until we both fell limp.

207 … I didn't think I had it in me. Jack said, "It's ectopic." He could see that I didn't know what 'ectopic' meant. I was excited that Honey could be carrying my baby. Jean went into the details. She described how a uterus was "Designed by God to release an egg from the ovary. The egg travels through the fallopian tube and into the uterus where it's fertilized." I assured them that I wasn't a moron. "That's not what happened," Jean added. "The egg was fertilized in Honey's fallopian tube." I could tell Jack was more uncomfortable with the situation than I was. He changed the subject. He said, "Honey told Jean that you proposed?" Their eyes were locked on me. It wasn't a moment to be shy or unsure of myself. "Yes, I did." Jean started to say something, but Jack interrupted her. "You see … the thing is … Henry ... we don't think that's a good idea. You are both still young. You have your whole lives in front of you. Life can take unexpected turns." He was challenging me. The Riders wanted to see if I would falter under pressure. They wanted me to balk, to prove how unfounded and fleeting my proposal was. I leaned in and looked them both squarely in the eyes. "Do you two remember falling in-love? Do you remember what it felt like to know that someone understood you? That someone *wanted* to understand you and grow old with you?" Jean stabbed a piece of French toast and dragged it through a small pool of maple syrup. It was sticky. She wasn't going to eat it, she needed something to occupy her hands as she offered me some "friendly advice." She said, "Maybe you could let Honey, *and us*, get through this ... *episode*. You're in school now. Wouldn't you rather concentrate on that? You should realize some of your dreams before you get married. Write that novel of yours. Experience life!

Because once you get married, all that ... *fun stuff* ... is over. *Marriage* is a *full-time job*. It's a long and seemingly never-ending series of problems and tasks. Is that what you want? Are you looking for *problems? Are you looking for trouble?*"

208 ... I felt like they were escorting me out of my own party. I understood. The Riders had to voice their opinion. Honey was their daughter. They couldn't see me in her future. From the moment she was born they had been envisioning a particular kind of life for her. It wasn't the idea of marriage they were opposed to. It was me. I didn't measure up. I wondered if I ever would. I said, "I appreciate your concern, but can't Honey make up her own mind? We're both adults." Jean scoffed at the challenge. She said, "Henry, she has been through a lot. With everything that's happened, with James. We just don't think now is the time." I didn't expect so much derision. Maybe that was naive of me. Jack wasn't saying much. I said, "What about you, Mr. Rider?" Jack touched Jean's hand and said, "I tend to agree with my wife." I was dumbfounded, really discouraged. Jean continued, "You'll be back in Rochester in no time. You can visit during your breaks. You'll see. This isn't the end of the world." All I wanted was a lousy smile, a handshake, a hug. Their daughter was happy, I was happy, and we were happy to chase after this dream. I had to stand up for myself. Opportunities for happiness don't come along often. I very calmly said, "I guess I don't see what you see. My proposal is serious. I love your daughter, and I want to marry her. I will marry her if she'll have me. I suppose that's something Honey and I will have to discuss, whenever she's ready. Right now, her health is what's important, not *our* personal plans for *her* life ... Thank you," I said, standing to leave. "For the water and the bacon."

209 … I promised James that once I left Rochester, I would never go back. It wasn't my fault that Honey had come to Iowa. James couldn't blame me for that. Neither could the Riders. She was in Iowa because she wanted to be in Iowa. That was the truth. I could see our future together. It wasn't filled with roses or softened by sunlight. It was real – filled with light and shadows, as real as anything could be between two broken people with an intricate past. I wanted Jack and Jean's support, but I didn't need it. There were just too many little risks doing it their way. I left the cafeteria and found a public telephone. I tried giving Dad a call, using the phone card he gave me. The line rang, but there was no answer. I hung up the phone. I was checking the change box for quarters when I heard a familiar voice. It was coming from an open door. There was a plaque on the wall. It read CHAPEL.

210 … The chapel carpet was a repeating pattern of gold and red – glory and the price for it. The pews were arranged to focus on a modest altar. On each unpresumptuous wall was one elaborate painting. Jason, the chaplain I met when the Riders arrived, was speaking to an older gentleman. They were looking at an effigy of Jesus hanging on a cross. It looked like he'd done it myriad times before, like it was his job, and he was tired of it. I tried to remember the last time I was in a church. It had been years. I must have looked like I was praying. In all honesty I was just trying to remember if, the last time I was in a church, it was for something good or something bad. I smiled and lifted my head. Jason was approaching. He said, "Henry, right? Is everything okay?"

211 ... I gave the chaplain the cliffs notes on Honey, the pregnancy, and the fall out from my proposal. Jason felt the weight I was carrying. He asked if I wanted to get my mind off of it for a moment. I followed the chaplain to the altar. He said, "Henry, I'd like to introduce you to Dr. David Pinkerton, the spiritual services administrator for the hospital. David, this is Henry." David stood poised in gray slacks, a loud salmon colored jacket over a black clerical shirt. We shook hands. His grip was fishy. Jason said, "Henry knows the young lady whose parents I met this morning. Maybe he could help us figure this out?" David and Jason looked at the effigy of Jesus hanging behind the altar. David said, "When you look at this print, what do you see Henry?" It was a portrait of a dying man. The son of God or not, I said, "It's a gruesome display of power." Jason smiled. David was focusing on the effigy. "It's an Albrecht Dürer," he explained. "I don't imagine you know who he is?" I interlocked my hands. "No," I said. I was about to get a lecture. David sang Dürer's praises, then Jason filled me in on their predicament. He said, "Can you see the penis?" I looked at Jason. David looked at Jason. This was not a joke. David said, "Well ... of course he's going to see the penis now!" I gave it another look. David didn't want to know what I thought. He said it was nice to meet me without meaning it and nodded in the chaplain's direction. "We can talk about this later," David said. Jason agreed. We watched David exit the chapel. Then he looked me square in the eye and asked, "You can see it, can't you?" We both looked at the effigy of Jesus. It was as plain as sunrise. "Totally."

212 ... Jason was funny. I'm sure he's still at the hospital. He had a new contract. He was already regretting it. He arranged the altar for a service and unloaded on David. The Jesus effigy had eaten up the signing bonus David promised Jason. "There were some beautiful places that offered me work, St. Mary's, Sarah Lawrence," Jason said. "I hate to admit it, but the money swayed me. Now I've got *this penis* hanging over my head." The chaplain moved around the altar finding additional distractions. He

reached into a bag and unrolled two sashes on one of the altar tables. "Listen to me! You came in here for something and I'm the one venting. What can I do for you, Henry?" I asked why he'd followed "the path of a priest." The chaplain liked the question. "Ah," he said. "I guess you find out, somewhere along the way what you're good at. I guess I'm just good at God."

213 ... I was asking questions, killing time when I should have been saving it. Chaplain Jason said, "Asking who wrote the Bible is kind of like asking who wrote the Qur'an, or the Torah? They were interpreters of the human condition. It was usually an elite club of educated *men* who wanted to create a lasting polemic." Jason moved a tray of small decanters and a chalice from a pedestal to the altar. "Jesus was a student of the polemic." I asked if he didn't mean to say that Jesus was "The teacher." Jason suggested otherwise. He said, "The gap in Jesus' whereabouts, through adolescence and early adulthood, supports the theory. If Jesus went to study, as we go through high school and college, the only people who could teach were the monks. He would have had to study at a seminary, or a holy place. This is where the books were. The monks controlled the libraries, translated texts. They taught the history and evolution of humanity using religion as their vessel. When Jesus' apprenticeship was completed, he began to teach, which is exactly what he was trained to do. Jesus was able to sew the more fashionable concepts of multiple philosophies into a robe of instructions that he promoted very successfully ... but then you see what fame gets you." I asked the chaplain how God fit into all of it. He said, "*That* is the million-dollar problem. God is no longer an outside entity? The human species has focused so much time and energy on believing that there is something else out there that we have literally altered our physiology into accepting the possibility that there is such an entity, that there is something else we all share when we shed these bodies, and that the only way to get there is by following a set of laws ... *written by men*. People live and die for ideas every day. Everyone thinks they have discovered the way to explain this shared absurd reality. In the end, we all *hope* we have

the right answer. We *hope* we've chosen the *right* path to paradise. Some people believe their path is the only one. Others see multiple paths. It's up to each of us to see what we want to see. In that, I think we are a hopeful animal. I hope that you see what I see. Because two are stronger than one. Four are stronger than three ... and ...." the chaplain paused and looked at the effigy of Jesus. He said, "So it seems, a mob is stronger than a man."

214 ... I sat in a pew for a few more minutes and thought about things. The chaplain was setting up for a service. He fetched a black box and a Bible from the back room of the chapel. In my mind, Honey's nod was confirmation enough. We would get married. Some day. Eventually. The chaplain set the box and Bible on the altar and blessed it. "I'm curious," he said. "Is there a reason Honey's parents don't want you to marry their daughter?" I told the chaplain, "I wasn't always a good kid." That seemed to be enough of an answer for him. Someone came into the chapel. The chaplain welcomed them as he stepped from the altar. There was a piece of me that wanted Jack and Jean to believe in me, the new me, the real me. I stood up to leave as the chaplain approached. He smiled. "There are a lot of potential questions, Henry. A man can drive himself crazy with the possibilities. The only question that I think you need to ask yourself is *Do you love her?*" I tried to answer, but he shooshed me. "Ask yourself: If today was my last day on Earth, would I want to spend it with Honey? You are young, Henry. Whatever your answer is, whatever happens, you've got your whole life ahead of you."

215 ... I was looking at an issue of Sports Illustrated when the doctor walked into the waiting room. Jack was letting Jean rest. She was laid

out on one of the couches. "Mr. Rider?" Something in the doctor's eye put Jack into an immediate and focused posture. The doctor asked if he might speak freely in front of me. Jack asked me to step out. I understood. I wasn't going to make a fuss. The sooner they knew how Honey was, the sooner I would know. Jack woke Jean. I remember stepping across the threshold of carpet onto the bright hallway tile as Jean released a confused shriek of horror. A chill ran through me like water down a wall. "No, no, no," Jean shouted. Jack barked, "What do you mean *complications*?!"

216 ... I dealt with it the only way I knew how. I fainted.

217 ... A nurse was holding my hand in the hallway. She was saying something but I could only hear Jack. He was comforting Jean in the waiting room. The astonishment continued to swell. It was the ocean. I was sinking into something so absolutely dark and far-way-cold, and the weight of it was crushing. Jack was staying afloat somehow, maybe with a little help from his years on the police force. Over time, I guess you probably see some shit, but everyone has a breaking point. Jack's was Honey. Jean said something inaudible and Jack shouted, "My darling girl!"

218 ... One of the other nurses approached me cautiously. I was a mess.

She said, "You're the fiancé right?" It was difficult for me to articulate my feelings in that moment. All I could do was nod. She bent down and whispered, "Would you like to see her?"

219 ... The nurse led me to Honey. There were no instruments or tables with tools in the room. Honey lay motionless, vacant, respectfully tucked in under a blue sheet on a cooling board. Her eye lids were partially closed. Her jaw was distended. The shimmering black liquid in her eyes had gone gray. It looked to me as if she'd seen the face of God. There was awe in her expression. Her skin was cold and pale. I kissed her lips and touched her chin. I drew my hand along her fingers, knuckles and wrist. The IV marks would never scar. There would be no child, no marriage. No matter how I wished I could change things, the universe was expanding. Time would continue to carry me away from this moment at an untold speed. There was nothing left to build on, nothing to pursue. What Honey and I had was as much as it would be, as far as we could go together, the most we could lose. There was a light tapping on the door. The nurse entered the room. There was no more time for good-byes. No more time to assess the situation. I asked the nurse what happened. She said, "I can't talk about it. Hospital policy." She led me into a hallway, then another. The hospital was a maze. I was a slow, but certain explosion. I needed air. I needed to vent.

220 ... I was madMadMAD. I tore something off the wall. The whole damn place needed to come down. I was trapped in the rubble of my own escape plan. The whole time I'd been chasing my tail, digging down when I should have been growing up. I needed to get away. I had to keep mov-

ing. All eyes were on me. Someone was calling after me. A set of stairs led to an exit. I slammed the door open and roared out into the rain. "Hey," someone shouted. "Get your ass back here!" I turned to face whoever it was. It was a security guard. "Calm down, sir! I saw you damage that fire safety device in the hallway upstairs. Whether you like it or not, you're coming with me." *Another cop*, I thought. Another fucking rule, another obstacle. I wanted to destroy him. The nurse arrived, she doused the situation. She called him by name, adding, "His fiancée just died. Give him some rope."

221 ... I was swollen with regret. What I wouldn't give for a little more time with Honey. There was a vicious knot in my stomach. I was shivering, soaked. I knew it was raining, that I was standing in it, but I hadn't realized it completely. The nurse was waiting for a visible moment of clarity. She asked me if I wanted to go somewhere. It was all I could say, "I want to go home."

222 ... The nurse led me to a small lounge with six chairs and a fake plant. She handed me a pale blue plastic cup of water and said, "I'm going to stay with you." In my mind, I could hear the exit music for a film. The feelings were unutterable. I just kept shaking my head, wiping the tears away, wondering how and why it all went so very wrong. Eventually, the nurse couldn't stay. She had things to attend to. I would have to deal with the pain in my own time, in my own way. No one was going to wave a wand over this situation and reorder the chaos. Honey was not coming back. I wanted so badly for someone to tell me this was all just a plot point. If only I had disappeared completely. Instead, I left a trail of bread

crumbs that led Honey to my door. Now, the end of this story had a very dark reality. "James is going to kill me."

223 … I was handed a prescription for another anti-epileptic drug called Rufinamide. The doctor wanted to follow up with me in a week. He seemed genuinely concerned as he handed me the release forms to sign. He said, "Call me if you have *any* side effects. We'll hone in on your specific dosage over the next couple of months." Focusing on the future was out of the question. I agreed with everything he said just to get the hell out of there. The Riders had Honey. They were going to take her body home. I had to walk back to the dorm. Campus was quiet, empty, a shell. It was early. Anyone in their right mind should have been sleeping in, taking it easy, re-booting. The river was stirring because it had to. The other natural elements seemed static. I went up the back stairs to the third floor of Currier Hall. *The Daily Iowan* was on the floor in front of N333. I used my keys to open the door and kicked the newspaper into the room. The door swung open, heavy. The fan was spinning in the window. A draft picked up the random papers and Honey's letters and pulled them across the floor like sleds moving in reverse toward the far wall. The floor was slick with furniture polish. Miscellaneous toys and knickknacks were scattered around the room. I remembered the break dancing routine, the laughter, the adrenalin. I was sore, tense, exhausted, and paranoid. I could retrace this pain back years. This was no hangover, it was my life. I closed the door behind me and picked up the newspaper and set it on the desk. I had jet lag in my own country. My eyes were closing on me. They were dry, achy, but I could read the headline of *The Daily Iowan*. "IC Cops: Girl's death ruled accidental." The article was a theoretical retelling of Honey's last 24 hours. Currier Hall was named, but the paper had spared my identification. I was "an un-named acquaintance, a male university student." Anyone could have put two-and-two together. Enough people saw Honey get rushed out of my room. It was only a matter of time before word got around. I picked up the telephone handset and dialed the numbers I needed to dial. The line was open. No one answered. I reset the handset. The

phone rang.

224 … It sounded pressing, though I suspected nothing would ever truly feel urgent again. Death changes a person's perspective on a great number of things. It is an inflexible happening, like a knock on a door. I entered the Dormitory Director's office. The woman behind the desk smiled and said, "Henry? I'm Julie Herst. Thank you for taking the time to speak with me." I told her that I didn't think I had a choice. Julie asked me to sit in a chair across from her. There was a large desk between us. I was convinced that I was being called to account for what happened in N333 with Honey. I was going to be evicted. Life would change again. For now, though, I'd reached a plateau. The lay of my life spread out around me. It was all there if I wanted to see it. Instead, I was looking at my feet. They were twitching. Julie started with small talk, adding "I'm sorry for your longer-than-normal stay in temporary housing. It's been an extraordinary couple of weeks. We haven't been able to place people as quickly as we would have liked." She paused. I wasn't going to add anything to the small talk. "So?" I said. "What's up?" Julie was taken off guard. She was used to people quivering in her presence. "Right," she said. Julie used a remote control to switch on a small television. "When we restored the dormitory, we added a security system," she started. I was convinced Officer Dunn had turned me in for grooving the snacks from the vending machines. I focused on the television. The ten seconds of video was clear. I walked into what was now Julie's office and stole the box fan for the Stanley Lounge. Julie said, "Is there any reason I shouldn't believe that's you?"

225 … I countered the very obvious fact that I had stolen the fan with a

question about privacy. Julie wasn't taking flack that day. Sweet enough on the outside, this little cookie was angry on the inside. She said, "Can you see why the cameras might be useful?" It wouldn't do me any good to fight this one. She set the remote control on the desk. "Can you explain why you thought it was okay to take the fan?" It was one of those stories that took very few sidesteps. There were nine guys in a largely unventilated glass and concrete room. The temperatures rose to over 105°F. I begged for a fan. No one helped us. So, I did something about it. Julie was disarmed by the story. She said, "Did you ever think to buy a fan? They're like ten bucks." She made a gesture, "I guess not. Thank you for your honesty." I told her I wasn't trying to pull anything over on anyone. She asked if I still had the fan. It was the one in the window of N333. I told her I left it in the Lounge when I got my room assignment. I said I could look for it, but I wasn't making any promises. She said, "If it's not in my hands by the end of the day, I'll need compensation, and I would have to write you up. It would be best for both of us if you found it." I stood and walked to the door, saying "As long as you understand why I took it." She said, "You were obviously very warm. I'll speak with the staff about it." She paused. "One other thing, Mr. Nighteen. I'm sorry to hear about your friend."

226 ... I weighed the truth and consequences of my recent past – a missing fan versus my best friend's death. I opened N333 to a very real figment of James pointing a handgun at me. He said, "Hello Henry" and pulled the trigger. I could smell the gunpowder as the apparition faded. It was a symptom of my guilt, a last grab from the *wash* as it fell into an abyss of sobriety. I know I will pay for Honey's death. I know that I will pay for the things I've been involved with, the people I've hurt. The trouble is not knowing how or when that debt will be called in.

227 … N333 was a disaster, a metaphor for how brittle things had become. I wanted to put everything back together. I wanted to organize the chaos. I started with Honey's letters. Her clothes. I put a barrette in her bag. There was a sketchbook inside. I looked at a few of the drawings: the exterior of a bus depot; the silhouette of a woman with a background of lockers; the aisle seats and profiles of passengers on a Greyhound bus headed toward an expanding horizon; a rotating cooler for pies at the end of a long diner counter, a jukebox in the distance. Honey was talented. That much, I knew. There was a ring of keys at the bottom of her bag. There were more key chains and pendants than keys: hearts and a monkey; a bottle opener; a small spoon; a cake; a stitched leather gingerbread man. There was a hard-pack of cigarettes with a lighter inside. I lit one and turned the fan on. There was a makeup case at the bottom. The fabric of the bag smelled like Honey. Like fireflies in a jar, I wanted to capture her scent, her flashes of illumination. But then there we would be, trapped under another heavy lid. As long as I was in that room, in that building, on that campus, in that city, in Iowa, I was going to associate it with the end of Honey's buoyant life. I looked around the room, at my personal effects that only a few short weeks ago I couldn't leave Rochester without. It all seemed so unimportant now. The clothes, the art, the books, the PowerBook … None of it was vital to what I had found in Iowa. The question was, "Where to from here?"

228 … I turned Honey's mix tape over and pressed PLAY. Her voice was soothing and painful. I sat down at the desk and lifted the receiver. The line was open. This time Dad answered. He was sighfully happy to hear from me. I found calm in his voice, in his patience. He said, "What's happening?" It was the most difficult thing I've ever had to tell one of the most important people in my life. "Honey's dead, Dad." He asked me to repeat myself, to explain what happened. I said, "I just can't." I let the words sink in. The steps he took toward acceptance were painful to expe-

rience over the telephone. Both of us were treading emotions in a storm. "Wow," he sighed, finally. "How can I help?" I didn't want to be the one to tell James. I asked Dad to get a message to him. I told him that Jack and Jean were bringing Honey home," I said. "When are you coming home?" he asked. I didn't know what I was doing. I was still thinking of escaping to Hollywood, but I was fragile, a cooling piece of glass ... you want to let me cool down before moving me. I asked Dad to be my emissary. I said, "I don't think I can do it. I don't think I can come home." He paused, then said, "You're coming home, Tip. You're going to honor your friend."

229 ... I felt like a kid again, doing what I'm told rather than what I think I should do. I huffed and puffed and kicked a few things, but eventually I had a bag packed. I shifted the weight of it as I stepped into the hall. I took one long look at the room before closing and locking the door. The last memory I have of N333 has a thought attached: that damn fan is still in the window and I'm pretty sure Julie saw me, as the bus that would take me to the airport shoved the curb. I went to the back of the bus, and set my bag on the seat beside me. I was the only pedestrian. The driver was playing metal music on a small stereo. The speakers were blown. He was looking at me in the mirror, drumming and driving. I pursed my lips and raised my eyebrows to engage and disengage him simultaneously. Somewhere near the library, he said, "MegaDETH!"

230 ... The agent at the Cedar Rapids Airport counter looked at my ID and booked me in first class. She said, "It looks like we oversold *economy*. It was our error. It's the only seat available." I said something about tardiness being one of my new virtues and she handed me the ticket. I boarded the plane and found my seat. It was roomy, comfortable, and blue. I hate flying, but if I had to do it this was the way to go. It didn't hurt that the

woman sitting next to me was actually pleasant. She smiled when we exchanged *Hellos*. When she sat down, she opened a small briefcase and removed some files. I looked out the window at the tarmac. It was going to be a short trip. All I had with me was Honey's backpack, a few clothes, Honey's letters and her sketchbook. While the crew prepared the plane. I studied Honey's drawings. There was a section of elaborate stacks of cakes. I could smell Honey in the pages. I brought the crease of the book to my face and drew in her scent. The woman sitting next to me gave me a curious look. I told her, "It's intentional. The drawings are scented. The artist is a chef." She was interested, but not enough to smell the sketchbook. I remembered watching Honey while she worked on some of the drawings. I admired how she could get so much on the page without scoring the paper. One curiosity was the repeating strands of pearls. Each string seemed to rise and fade from the viewer. Honey had included them on several of the envelopes and letters she sent to me in Iowa. The letters were in her backpack. I considered re-reading them, examining her handwriting, cross-referencing the pages in her notebook with the themes of each letter. I was sure something more could be made of it, but an outline on one of the pages of the sketchbook caught my attention. It was a key. I remembered what Honey said as they wheeled her toward surgery. There was a hiding place in her room, under the carpet. I was flipping through the pages faster now. I had to get there. This was my new urgency ... just as having her once was.

H O M E

231 ... It was evening when I arrived in Rochester. I had not slept on the plane. Dad met me at the gate. His embrace was stronger than I remembered. I almost asked him to stop hugging me. He let go and grabbed my face. "I love you," he said. It was as if I were watching him from some deep tunnel inside my own body. "I love you too," I said. "People were watching us. Can we go home now?" Dad carried my bag to the car. I expected he would begin asking questions the moment we were alone. He is a private man. He doesn't enjoy shaking the dirty laundry where others might notice. What were we supposed to say? Who was supposed to say it first? What took precedence? Dad put the keys in the ignition and hoped the car would start. When it did, he said, "Buckle up, you're not in Iowa anymore."

232 ... The old house was a welcome sight. The big maple tree out front was dropping leaves on the lawn. Dad pulled into the driveway and gave me a wide berth on the passenger side. He carried my bag. The white concrete step at the bottom of the gray front porch stairs was a finish line of sorts. I made my way past it and took a deep breath when we walked in the front door. The house smelled of fresh potpourri and exposed wood. I could smell the books in the front study. Dad carried my bag upstairs. I followed him. He turned my bedroom light on and offered to make us

some tea. The moment he left, I collapsed on my bed. I vaguely remember Dad coming back with the tea but I was already asleep. He set the mug down and covered me with a blanket. He turned off the light and faded to a silhouette in the doorway. He whispered, "I hope you have a child some day, so you can understand how much I love you, Tip. It's good to have you home."

233 ... That night, I had a dream about Dad. He was a young boy, playing along a creek with his friend – my nick-namesake – *Tip*. The details of the dream and the details of Tip's story are blurry, but certain. Dad went home for dinner while Tip continued to play at the creek. Tip had epilepsy. He had a seizure, fell into the water, and drowned. I woke when Dad opened the curtains the next morning. The light was blinding, grey. I felt like I had slept a lifetime. Dad said, "You should eat something before we go." I asked him where we were going. "You slept through the night. It's tomorrow afternoon. The Riders are having friends and family to the house in a little while." I was alert enough to ask if it was *a wake*. Dad wasn't sure if Honey would be there or not. "The funeral is tomorrow," he said. The words landed heavy. "You should wear something nice."

234 ... Supper was soup. Dad made the soup himself. He made croutons in the toaster with some white sandwich bread and a little herbed olive oil. It was nice to have some home cooking. We ate at the table, instead of on the couch in front of the Tv. We were both wearing slacks, shirts, and neckties. "What's with all this?" I asked, referring to the soup and croutons. Dad was proud of what he'd made. He explained his "renewed interest in leading a healthier lifestyle with a diet rich in vitamins, natural fats, veggies

and proteins." Only weeks earlier, we spoke about the benefits of a frozen pizza, wearing sweats and sitting on the couch. Something was up. I was only kidding when I said, "What's her name?" He thought my observation was "Very astute. You'll like Donna. I should warn you," he added. "She's a screamer. Not in the sense that you're thinking. She screams at everything. When she laughs. When she gets surprised. Pretty much all the time." I asked if she was coming to the Riders' with us. Dad said, "That probably wouldn't be a good idea." It was a disarming moment. We both laughed a little. "Dig in," he said.

235 ... The drive to the Riders was difficult. Innocence can fill all kinds of spaces if you just give it a push. I guess I'd lost it somewhere. Dad and I had several almost-conversations, but we were going to my best friend's death party. How jovial could we get? How much small talk was there between "your best friend is dead" and "it looks like you are at least partially to blame." Dad turned the car onto Edgerton Street and parked a few doors down from the Riders. He said, "How do you want to work this?" I asked him what he meant. He was meeting with the new girlfriend. He said, "I'll pay my respects tomorrow. Do you want me to come back to pick you up?" I told Dad I'd find a way home. "I'm sorry, Tip. I know it's a bad excuse, but Donna got these tickets a long time ago." Time, I guess, is relative.

236 ... Jack and Jean were greeting guests as they arrived. They welcomed me as Dad drove off. Jean suggested I enjoy the refreshments inside. There were people lined up behind me. Their friends were my strangers. I had to think I was only there because of a clause in the Riders agreement with

their daughter. The house was ornamented with photos of Honey, but Honey was not there. It felt strange to be in the house, sober. There was a bowl of punch with fruit floating in it and cookies on a platter. Loitering from one photo of Honey to another was heartbreaking. Thankfully, I found Raine in the back yard. He was smoking a cigarette. He looked spent. We shook hands and hugged. I offered him a cookie. He chose one with rainbow sprinkles and said, "Lynnae's not coming. She said she couldn't handle it." I told him I understood, "How are you holding up?" I asked. Raine knew Honey for most of his life. I was sure he was struggling, but he deferred his answer by saying, "You look good." The only good thing about being home was that I had gotten some rest. I had a decent meal and a shower. I didn't feel winded or confused or lost. I wasn't looking for anyone's approval. I knew I wouldn't get it. I felt like I had been reset, sent back to the beginning. This might have been the wrong thing to feel in that moment, but Honey's home was my home away. Cops or no cops, just being there put me at ease. I think I sighed. Raine brought me out of it. He said, "What the fuck happened in Iowa?"

237 … Raine and I found a quiet spot on the stairs to talk. He had a plate of food in his lap. He was drinking from a can of ginger ale. He was okay for the moment. I wasn't. Telling Raine about Iowa only made me want to investigate more. *A hiding place under the carpet.* I repeated the phrase to myself and looked around. The coast was clear. "Cover me?" I said. Raine raised his can of ginger ale in agreement. I climbed the stairs to the second landing. Honey's bedroom door was closed. I opened it. The two windows were open. The curtains were moving in the breeze. It felt like years since I'd been there. The room smelled like incense and Honey. I tried to take in as much of it as possible. My lungs were weak. There were red and white COOL stickers stuck to items around the room. I eyed the one on the corner of the carpet … but someone was coming. I heard Raine say, "Upstairs." It was Jack. He entered Honey's room as I picked up a Buffalo Springfield CD. He said, "Can I help you, Henry?" I showed him the CD and said, "This was Honey's favorite. Raine and I were hoping we could play it."

Jack sighed. Living with a cop's intuition is probably exhausting. "Sure," he said. "Bring it. Jean wants to cut the cake."

238 ... Jack closed Honey's bedroom door and escorted me to the living room. Several people had already assembled around Jean and a cake in the dining room. She was emotional but clear. Jean said, "Somehow, Honey knew this day would come. She knew that we would be here without her. And," Jean sobbed for a moment. She regained her composure and continued. "When Honey was five-years-old, my Great Aunt Agnes passed. She had a modest church service. There was a buffet in the church basement afterward. Honey didn't like the food they were serving. It was what the church could afford. Well, Honey had a tantrum of sorts...." Jean laughed and swelled and sighed. "Honey screamed at the top of her lungs, '*When I die, I want cake*!'" The attendants erupted in laughter. Jean smiled and said, "Honey wanted us to eat cake ... So, we're having cake." Someone said, "Special girl."

239 ... It was a sober and sobering night. Raine and I managed to maintain a low-key status, moving to specific places around the Rider home that reminded us of the fun times we all had together. Eventually, we ran out of memories and started focusing on the present. Whatever that feeling is, when you've loved and lost someone, it was awful to feel and it was difficult to watch. It passes, I know. But the feeling roots itself in the shirt-pocket of the soul. Raine and I left the Riders together and crossed the street. He had been using the neighbor's house as a thoroughfare to get to Honey's house since he was young. We shook hands and hugged and said we'd see each other at the funeral. Then Raine disappeared into the dark-

ness. It had been a complex night. I was looking forward to the long walk home. But what began as an intellectually painstaking loop of un-rightable wrongs was now a throat-swelling paranoia as James stepped from behind a large tree into the lamp light. He said, "Hello ... *sick* boy."

240 ... I didn't know whether to run or embrace him. I was speaking in half sentences and open-ended questions. James clarified the situation for me. "I escaped. Honey's not in there, is she?" I told him she wasn't. "Is there any food left?" he asked. I listed some of the things I had eaten. "You escaped?" I said. James looked at the house. Jack and Jean were sitting in the living room with a few straggling guests. He said, "Stay put. I'll be back." He disappeared into the shadows behind Jack and Jean's house. I was scared and confused, mumbling questions under my breath. *Why the fuck was he out? What the hell was he doing?* I took a few paces up the street, to stay out of sight. It was a long few moments but James reappeared. He was carrying a plate. He had a big piece of cake. He was curious, "Who the fuck has cake at a wake?" He dug his fingers deep into the frosting and pulled off a hunk of the almond-flavored breading. I told him that Honey wanted us to have cake when she died. James ate the cake, licked his fingers, and gave the idea a shrug. "She *was* a *weird* bird, *wasn't* she?"

241 ... I was nervous, I guess it showed. I set the bottles of beer on the counter and looked at the closed circuit televisions behind the cashier. James was avoiding every one of the cameras. The cashier picked up on my anxiety. He asked if everything was okay and bagged the beer. I had put him on alert. I was sure there was a gun behind the counter. The ca-

shier was prepared to use it. He gave me a receipt and my change. I never even saw the guy's face but I'm sure he could pick me out of a lineup. There was a height scale on the door. It was the type of place that gets robbed enough to warrant its own system of averages. I walked out and very casually looked around the parking lot for James, for police. It wasn't until I started doubting that I had seen James at all that he reappeared. This was not some hallucination. This *was* happening.

242 … It was late. There was a guy coming out of Monty's Crown. He was smashed, wearing jeans and a flannel. James offered a couple of our beers in exchange for a ride. Then James convinced the guy to let him drive. The guy loved the idea. He handed James the car keys and we got into a small two-door hatchback. James started the car and put it in gear. I handed him a beer and asked where we were going. "Where *are* we going?" the drunk repeated. James said, "*The High Point.*" The drunk asked what *the High Point* was. "Is that where you guys get high? Are you guys *holding*?" He hiccuped. I gave him a beer. James looked at the drunk intently. "It's where we're going to kill you," James said. The drunk couldn't have gotten more afraid more quickly. It was hilarious. "Wow," James said. "I'm fucking with you! Do we look like murderers?" The drunk gave us a once-over, already trapped several miles into his future. "No," he laughed. "You look *straight* to me." I couldn't help myself. I said, "It's always the normal ones you have to look out for." The drunk laughed. He was still trying to get a read on us. Then, whatever it was, something changed. The drunk started panicking. He said, "Wait, wait, wait. You guys aren't seriously going to kill me, are you?" James took his eyes off the road and said, "I'm *seriously* considering it." The drunk got quiet. It only made James' maniacal laughter more contagious.

243 … James stopped the drunk's car in the middle of Kendrick Road and got out. He left the door open and didn't set the parking break. The car started to roll. The drunk was asking questions, but there was no sense answering him. I got out of the rolling car. James had vanished. If I didn't know where he was going, I wouldn't have been able to follow him into the dark. I couldn't see him, but I could hear him ahead of me on the canal trail. The water in the canal smelled of a season of boating. The air was muggy. It made me thirsty. I opened another beer and drank deeply. In the distance, I could see the frame of the guard gates and the large steel partition that dropped into the water to seal the lock. As I walked along the canal path, the holes in my memory were filled with images of innocent summer afternoons spent leaping from the High Point into the shimmering sunlit canal. Now it was night and the nostalgia was all too dark and bittersweet.

244 … It was difficult knowing the last time James and I were at the High Point together Honey was with us. If I close my eyes, I can still see her, sitting on the edge of the higher wall, sopping wet, in shorts and a white t-shirt, a beacon of sunlight reflecting in the puddles of the slab around her. I spliced images and days together as I climbed the scaffolding toward the top. There were many rungs and platforms we practiced leaping from as we worked our way up, until finally we were all leaping from the High Point on a regular basis. We never went to the top if we weren't going to jump. I expected James wanted to honor Honey with one more leap. I could anticipate the fall as I climbed the framing. I had vertigo halfway up. The breeze on the ground was a wind at the top. There was very little protection up there, it was just a catwalk and some framing. But the view was killer.

245 ... James was leaning against one of the supports at the top of the High Point. There were two beers left. I handed him one. I said, "You can see the jail from here." James said, "That's why I'm facing *this way*." The direction James was looking, the espresso black canal faded to dark blue in the distance. To the left, the highway played a repetitive whoosh in orange light. "To Honey, ay?" We touched our beers together and drank deeply. "So," I said. James interrupted me, "I got out in the laundry. One of the guards helped me. I've gotta do him a favor now." James paused. It was one of those long uncomfortable pauses where nothing can, but everything usually does, go wrong. James said, "And now you're back." I told him that it wasn't something I chose to do. "You should have stayed there," he added. "You should have stayed in Iowa." I knew James well enough to know when I could push back. "I didn't have a choice," I said. "I had to come home. Otherwise ... You know ... Why the fuck did I have to go away? Why did *I* have to run?" It was a lot of questions that had no answers. James relaxed. He said, "I never wanted you to go down for the shit I did." I told him that wasn't the way I heard it. "Why don't you tell me what you heard and how you heard it then?" I drank from my beer. It was bitter and sudsy, not at all refreshing. "W-well," I stammered. "It felt like you were trying to keep me away from Honey." James guffawed. He said, "Can you blame me?"

246 ... I couldn't fault James for wanting to keep Honey to himself. I would have done the same thing. I would have tried to protect her from threats. I can see how I might have appeared like a threat. James said, "A lot of good any of that did. She played me pretty good. I had no idea Honey had such strong feelings for you. I guess I freaked." I asked him what he meant. He said, "When she told me she was going to Iowa, I punched her. Right in the gut. That was the last time I saw her. I got a week in soli-

tary for it. That's when I planned to get the fuck up outta that place. Now look at me! I'm on top of the world!" James was very proud of himself. I let the story sink in. It warmed my engine. My engine got hot. I must have bitten my lip. I tasted blood. "She got between us," James said. "Now we can get back to it." I threw my beer as far as I could and said, "Back to what? Honey is dead! You didn't know she was pregnant ... did you?"

247 ... James did not know that Honey was pregnant. They were hard words for him to hear. They were hard words to say. I let the long sentences and descriptions fade to silence while I opened another beer. James finished his beer and threw the bottle into the darkness. "Well, what's done is done," he said. I couldn't believe how laid back he was about it. We had both spent a quarter of our lives with Honey and I couldn't help but blame him for what had happened. I confronted him. I said, "*What's done is done*, because you hit her. You killed that girl. You killed that baby." James was dumbfounded. He had never seen this side of me. "Let it go," he said. "Do you think that kid was yours? Let *me* tell *you* something, *H*. Honey was a whore! Who knows whose kid it was?! Even if it was one of ours, imagine the monstrosity of it. If it *was* my fault, I did everyone a favor." That was the last veil. All I saw was red. I said, "Honey wasn't a whore! She loved us. She cared about us." James repeated himself slowly, "Big, big whore." I threw my beer at him. He ducked and I shoved him. James said, "You don't want to do this, H. Not up here." I shoved him again. I said, "What are you afraid of? You think you're hard-core? You're not dangerous, you're just mean." James took a step back. He could see this might not go well for either of us. James was trying to diffuse the situation. He said, "She ran to you in the end. I'll give you that. But there are things about each of us that no one will ever know. Sometimes, some of those dark secrets get discovered! Sometimes the light gets in! Can we agree on that?" Maybe James was right. Maybe I had won Honey's love. Maybe this was enough of a small victory. I looked through the steel frame of the guard gate at the canal below. There was no going back. I approached him with my hand extended and said, "Bros before hos?"

James smiled. We shook hands. It was one of those elaborate handshakes that ended in a deep-wrist embrace. A handshake so strong I was able to swing him out over the water before he could anticipate the need to secure himself.

248 ... The moment will last forever if only for the lack of proof. The only things keeping James and I from falling were my grip and his toe-holds. I had never seen him so scared. I was confident in my strength. I could have held him there for hours. "Tell me," I said. "Do ... *not* ... let me go!" The air was cool in that moment. His grip was stretching the skin on my arm. His fingertips were searching the bones in my wrist for a better hold. "What does it feel like?" I said. "Do you miss her? Because I do. Did you ever really love her? I did. A whore? Really? How about this. You're the whore! You're the one that fucked us! How are you going to get yourself out of this one, James? You fucking killed Honey, man. You killed all of us ... Now it's your turn." I released my grip. James slipped. He said, "I'll fucking kill you H! Don't ... you ... *Fuck*!!"

249 ... I never heard a splash. My heart was in my throat. I could hear the blood washing around inside on a current of adrenalin as I panted and slowly realized what had happened. I searched the canal from the High Point. There wasn't so much as a rivulet. I climbed down the scaffolding and searched from the walkways, along the walls, up and down stream. I was horrified, scared out of my mind. I walked the gates. "Come out, come out, wherever you are." James had done this before, fooled us all by swimming upstream under water and hiding in the bushes until we were out of our minds with fear. This late in the season, with less and less boat

traffic in the canals, the mud settles and the water can be shallower than you'd think. There were times I jumped from some of the lower platforms and got stuck shin-deep in the mud. Still other times, I knocked into things people had thrown into the water, an anchor, cinder blocks, a refrigerator. You never really knew what was in the water when you jumped. I had to be sure. I jumped in, clothes and all. I swam into the black liquid, searching for a head of hair, an arm, anything, until I just couldn't look anymore. I swam back to the ladder. It was slick with moss. I almost didn't make it. That's not hyperbole. I had to wrap my arm around a rung to rest, otherwise I would have drowned too.

250 ... I ran back up the scaffolding to the High Point, searching the canal in both directions for any movement in the shadows and highlights. I was convinced James was fucking with me. Then, I was convinced that I had killed my best friend. I felt guilty, but I also didn't want to get caught. I collected the beer bottles and made sure the receipt from the grocery store was in the bag. I wiped the framing of the guard gate with my shirtsleeve, and rubbed the supports where I had secured myself to let James go. I was very precise and manic. I looked around for *any* evidence that would suggest we were there at all. There was only me. And then I left that place.

251 ... I made my way through the shadows, navigating the University of Rochester and the Mount Hope Cemetery darkness to Dad's house. Dad had company. There was a car in the driveway. The house was dark but for a soft light in his bedroom. I entered quietly and went to the basement to put my clothes in the drier. I added a few drier sheets. There was a basket of clothes on the floor. I put on some sweatpants and a t-shirt and took my

shoes outside to the clothes drier vent to dry. I was on autopilot. I let my habits take over and did what I normally do before bed. I made a bowl of cereal. I couldn't eat it. My stomach was in a knot. But at least it looked as though everything was in its right place. Then I remembered Dad's warning. His new girlfriend was a screamer. He wasn't kidding. She sounded like she was having a fit. I turned on *Aeon Flux* and tuned them out as best as I could. Eventually, Dad came down for a glass of water. He stood at the edge of the kitchen in his shorts and said, "I didn't know you were home. I'm sorry about *that*. Donna's staying the night. How did everything go?" What could I tell him? "It was sad."

252 ... I went to bed, but I couldn't sleep. I went over each fault, each scenario, each individual history, imagining how small changes could have made big differences. Thankfully, it started to rain. I imagined the pitter-patter of water on the bedroom window was also falling at the High Point. The footprints, any fingerprints were washing away. Ten-times-ten, I watched James' fall. I watched our rejoining embrace disengage. It was a great guilty pleasure. I felt like Honey's death had been vindicated. The question was, in a world of threes, between the nightmares and dreams, would there be another?

253 ... I knocked on the bathroom door. A female voice came from inside, "I'll be right out." I went down stairs. Dad was in the kitchen. He'd gotten fresh mums from the Floral Company next door. "I got these for Honey," he said. He was wearing a black suit. I paused at the refrigerator and said he and the flowers looked nice. I was wearing a suit, my oldest. My legs were shaking. I was as weak as tea, paranoid as butter. I opened a can of

soda as Dad's new girlfriend came down the stairs. Dad said, "Hel-lo! Donna, this is my son, Henry." She extended a hand and her condolences. She was thirty something, and not-too-difficult-to-look-at. As tasteless as it was, Donna's dress was complementary. Dad gave her one of Honey's mums and offered to make us breakfast. Donna dissuaded him and I went into the living room and turned on the Tv. The sportscaster was calling the scores from the previous night. The weatherman detailed the movement of several radar images. Then, the anchors ended the newscast on a story about school lunches. There was nothing about James, no news of a body being discovered. I checked the other channels too. It was still early though. No news wasn't exactly good news.

254 ... We were following the procession, the long way, into Mount Hope Cemetery. The rain veiled the windshield in small disasters. Each disaster was wiped away. As we drove along the river, we passed my old professor, Jaja Paduzzi. He was riding his bicycle. I considered blaming Jaja for everything as I scanned the scenery for James along the banks of the Heritage Trail. Jaja was no more to blame than Prudence. Poetry was not the culprit here. I was. It was awkward, Dad and Donna and I in the artificially hot car, commenting on the rain, the occasional bump, the local landmarks. Dad knows a lot about Rochester and the cemetery. He couldn't help sharing stories I'd heard many times before. Honey's flowers were on the back seat beside me. "Did you talk to James?" Dad asked. It was an innocent question that rendered me almost silent. "No," I said. Dad looked in the rearview mirror. I looked out the window. He said, "He and Honey dated for a long time. It's too bad he can't be here today." Donna asked why James couldn't come. Dad said, "He's incarcerated." Donna was taken aback. "Oh," she said. The quieter I was, the farther the truth might float away. I was going to exude distance and introspection, if only to maintain what little peace I had left in my heart. I was in mourning, my friend was dead after all.

255 ... Dad parked the car. The funeral director opened the back of the hearse. The rain was coming down in passing sheets. Jack and Honey's uncles carried Honey's casket toward a makeshift tent marked with chairs. Dad and Donna wanted to wait for a break in the rain to make their way to the tent. There would be no good time or bad time to move. The time was now. I stepped out in a torrent. The ground was soft. Raine was inside the flap. His eyes were bloodshot. He was high. I understood. I wished we were all as high as he was. We exchanged a simple handshake in which he passed something to me and winked. "You don't need much," he said. I put whatever it was in my pocket and walked toward Honey's casket with the mums. The faces that smiled at me naively the night before were now awash in suspicion. I was the boy who led Honey to this hard wood box and turf grass. I stood in line to deliver the flowers and a short prayer. As I approached Honey's casket, I could smell the cold damp earth wafting from the hole. Between the green straps on the mechanical crane I could see a puddle of muddy water at the bottom, a white wrapper floating in it. It was an unsettling curio, an imperfection I could not correct. I placed the mums on the wet casket and wondered why the Riders weren't allowing us to see Honey before they put her to sleep forever. I said a few words under my breath, in the fog of remorse, then found a seat near Raine. He was nodding off, flawlessly stoned.

256 ... Dad and Donna came into the makeshift tent as the preacher started. "It's difficult to lose someone who has obviously touched so many lives ... We have friends and family, and other loved ones here to honor Honey Rider today as she passes from this world into the next ... Death can be difficult for those of us left behind, especially when the deceased is plum with unspent potential. I understand from speaking with a lot of

you, how much Honey meant to you. I understand that Honey enjoyed the little things in life, like her rabbits and her dog, Rufus. As she grew older, Honey enjoyed the company of her friends and family, she enjoyed drawing and painting, and baking. I understand Honey was thinking about going to New York to study to be a pastry chef, and that she intended to travel to Paris one day ... Now, we are the ones charged with carrying those dreams forward ... There are many questions that come with death. Some of those questions, there will be answers for ... Some questions will never be answered ... The Lord's ways are mysterious. Because we do not know how the story ends, that should not mean that we lose faith. We should not live in darkness or fear. We should live in the light. *Love* prepares us for that light. *Love* carries the weight and *Love* shows us a path forward. *Love* leads us toward His Holy Kingdom." I was ready to vomit. It was way too saccharine. The preacher was brainwashed. Others at the service were nodding in agreement. Honey wasn't interested in religion. If she was aware of what was happening at her own funeral, she would have been really pissed off. It was wrong that Honey was taken. I didn't see the point in it. I just wanted her back. And I wanted the preacher to stop eyeballing me. But then he reached out. He invited *anyone* who wanted to speak to say *a few words*.

257 ... I looked at the Riders. Jack looked at me. His complete lack of expression was enough of an indicator that I should make it short and sweet. They would have preferred this moment to pass without incident. I had no interest in remaining silent. I was going to be myself, speak for myself, and stand up for myself. I started to speak from my small place on the surface of the earth. The preacher invited me to the front, beside the casket where I could smell the flowers, see the photos, be the focal point. I stood to the side of the podium and looked down at my shoes. They were as shiny as an 8ball. I offered a nervous laugh and said, "I bought these shoes three years ago at Midtown Mall with Honey. We skipped school one day. We were just goofing off. She saw the shoes in one of the windows and said, *Shoes really do make a man.* I honestly thought Honey meant she

would like me more if I bought the shoes. Her opinion meant a lot to me. So, I bought them, and ..." We went back to her house. We got high and James came over. He told me to take my shoes and go home. When I got home, I put the shoes in the closet. "I never wore them. Until today." No one could anticipate where this was going. Even I didn't know what I was getting at. The wind picked up. The flap at the back of the tent opened. In the distance, I could see James sitting on one of the tombstones like an eager gnome. The flap closed. I had completely lost my train of thought. I looked at Dad for inspiration. The tent shook and the flap opened again. James was smiling, encouraging me to continue with a repetitive gesture. The flap closed. I pointed and said, "I think someone's out there." Jack stood up and one of the other guests opened the flap. Jack stepped out. James was gone. Jack looked at me curiously. Dad looked at me, as did the rest of the guests, with concern. My hands were shaking. I was light-headed. I reached for the podium to steady myself, but reality and eternity were sharing colors in the black and white. Then, everything visible vanished, and there was only the pain of absolute silence.

258 ... For three days, I laid motionless. The machines were keeping me alive. My senses were unavailable. It would have been an uncomfortable way to spend an eternity.

259 ... Waking wasn't easy. It was as if I had come from nothing into a cloudy, sepia-toned hell. My head was throbbing. My arms were plugged with needles connected to tubes and bags of liquid. My right eye was bandaged, along with the rest of my head, but I could see Jasper. Jasper was ... more than enough ... for the moment.

260 ... "Welcome back," Jasper mumbled. His white body cast and bandages made him look like a ghost, in traction. Jasper was bandaged from head to toe, fingertip to fingertip. His predicament was disturbing. I was growing increasingly aware of my own. Jasper mumbled from inside the bandages, "Yer in the hospital." I didn't understand. I couldn't speak. I groaned instead. My monitors were eeping. Jasper said, "Yer fine." There was a hose across my face and something in my nose. I tried to remove it and pushed myself up in the bed, but I was no longer in control of my body. Jasper leaned in my direction. "Want me to call the nurse?" His speech was garbled. All sound was slow and analog. There was no separating the truth from the frustration. I was trapped. All I could do was nod and wait.

261 ... The nurse arrived. She was excited. "You're awake," she said. "I'm Becky." Becky offered me some crushed ice and called for the doctor. Jasper was looking at her ass. She had a nice figure but her face was a bad roll of the die. She helped me to get adjusted. She wiped the Vaseline from my eyes and a doctor came in. He was smiling, calm and confident. He said *Hello* to Jasper and to Becky and looked at my chart. "How's your head?" he said. I tried to articulate the pain but my tongue and cheek cramped. They could see I was having a hard time of it. The doctor said, "Everything's okay. Let's relax. Let's re-lax. This will pass. That's it. Everything's fine...." Over the next few minutes, he laid some awful big words and concepts on me, but everything made sense. I had a seizure. I hit my head. I dislocated my right shoulder. "You've been in a vegetative state for three days, Henry. I need you to understand something. It's

very important that you stay awake. Now that we have you back, we want to keep you here. This is just to let your brain re-set and find a normal rhythm." I acknowledged receipt of the transmission. "Okay, good. Jasper? Do you think you can help us keep Henry awake?" Jasper mumbled, "I can try."

262 ... News of my waking spread quickly. The nurses delivered flowers and read the cards. Whenever I tried to speak, my tongue, cheek and face cramped. The pain was horrendous. Only the most essential, basic sounds were available. The rest was pure pressure. Jasper was watching Tv. He had the remote. He's a fan of game shows. I tried to tune it out, to stay awake. I looked around the room, through the curtains in the window, and tried to count the holes in the acoustic ceiling panels. I wasn't sure what the trouble was that started all of this, but I had a pretty good feeling there were reasons I was in this can of worms.

263 ... It was exhausting trying to stay awake. Jasper did what he could by keeping the Tv volume set high, but somewhere in the cacophony of static and canned laughter I found enough solace to drift off.

264 ... I heard Dad's voice, but I could not see him. I was deep inside a

well of myself. The walls were too slick. I tried to climb toward his voice. He was repeating my name. Dad sighed when I opened my eyes. There was a modest bouquet on the bedside table. He touched my arm. He was smiling. My mouth was dry. I pointed at the Styrofoam cup of melting ice. Dad held the cup and spooned some of the ice into my mouth. The crunchy shavings melted. I licked my lips and pointed to the stick of lip balm on the bedside table. Dad took off the cap and puckered his lips as he applied the lip balm to mine. Life as an animated vegetable was not something I had figured into my equations. I prayed for an end to the doting. I reached for the bedside table. "More?" Dad said. "I'll go get some." I shook my head *No*. There was something else on the table. "The note pad?" Dad asked. I groaned and nodded again. Dad handed me the note pad and a pencil. It hurt too much to use my right hand. I used my left. "?happened"

265 ... Dad isn't a great storyteller. He gets right to the point. He said, "You got up to say something [at Honey's funeral]. You had a seizure. You took out one of the panels of the tent when you fell. There was a headstone on the other side. You hit the right side of your head. Thank god the hospital was across the street. They almost had to intubate you. It was horrible." Dad touched my arm. There were CaT scans done while I was in the coma. The swelling in my brain wasn't significant enough to warrant surgery. I was on oxygen, fluids, and "Mannitol," he said. "Prudence is coming from Alfred tonight. You'll be able to see her tomorrow." I didn't know who Prudence was. I wrung my eyebrows and cocked my head. "Your sister?" Dad said. "Do you remember your sister?"

266 ... Dad left when my food arrived. Ours was the last delivery, so I was able to convince the nurse to leave the cart in the room with us. It made the rest of the evening a little more bearable and interactive. Jasper had enough range of motion to rotate the cart. I had enough energy to write. He had a growing pile of notes on his bedside by the time we got to our desserts – red and green Jell–O. Jasper grunted something in my direction. It was very difficult to understand him. I understood it better the second time he asked, "Is she hot? Your sister? She good lookin'?" I shrugged. I barely remembered I had a sister let alone what she looked like. I finished another note and set it on the cart. Jasper read the note aloud, "?happened2U"

267 ... Jasper was fidgeting. He couldn't reach a picture frame beside his bed. He knocked it over and had to page Becky to help. Becky handed me the picture frame and went back to her station. It was a photo of a red barn, an advertisement that had been torn from a magazine. I set a note on the cart for Jasper. Jasper answered my comment slowly. "Yes. It's ... an ad ... Y'ever do any *fanning*?" I had never heard the term. Apparently, Jasper liked to sit in his rocking chair with a cup of gasoline under the seat. As he rocked back and forth, the air would stir the fumes. It was enough to "get a little dizzy." I didn't understand the connection to the ad. Jasper grunted, "I had a barn like that. I was fanning inside. I blacked out. It burned. I burned ... And *voila*!" I looked at the barn in the ad. It was easy to imagine it in flames. It was old and dry. It would have gone up quickly. Jasper said, "I'm ... my ... own ... friggin' billboard! ... for how ... to fuck up ... your life."

268 ... The doctor gave me the okay. I could sleep at will. It was one of the nicest things anyone's done for me in a long time. "I think we're past

the worst of it," he said. I ate a hearty meal and remember watching the MTV Video Music Awards as I drifted into the dark. That night, my dreams were set in post-Eisenhower America. Everything was black and white and manicured. It was peaceful even if I knew it wasn't true. I slept through the night and most of the morning. When I woke, there was a note in my hand. Jasper said, "She, just left, was here, all morning." I opened the note. *Brother, I didn't want to wake you. You are so special to me. I am in awe of you. I've always been in awe of you. I'll see you tonight. I'm going to Mom's for lunch. Be strong. - Prudence.* I closed my eyes and tried to imagine my sister's face, or my mother's. It was difficult, but not impossible.

269 ... Jasper rattled his traction, "Hey ... Wake up ... you're dreaming." I told Jasper, "They're memories." It was the first full sentence I had managed since the fall. It was the kick I needed. I wanted to get out of there. Stir crazy in a hospital is one thing. Stir crazy at home would be better. At least, if I was at home, I could go outside or something. I paged the nurse's station and drew a wheelchair on the note pad. I hoped for Becky, but one of the older nurses came in. I showed her the drawing. "You're good," she said, adding a battery of questions that all had the same answer. "Wheelchair."

270 ... The nurse asked which way. I pointed toward the first plaque I saw. "The Main Entrance?" I drew a sun with heat and light lines, closed my eyes and pretended to tan. I held my hands together as if to beg, but she mis-read the gesture. "You want to go outside to pray? Okay, let's make that happen." She pushed me through the hospital like it was her mission,

but her idea of a comfortable place outside was not my idea of a comfortable place outside. She led me to the entrance on Elmwood Avenue and stopped short of the sidewalk. The awning created a broad shaded environmentally ergonomic space. She locked my wheels and sat behind me on a bench, cross-legged, and checked her watch. The buses and patients and staff came and went. It was fresh air, but it was canned fresh air. I asked the nurse if we could go a little further, into the sunlight. She seemed to think it was best if I stay cool. I didn't think that I was that bad off. Was sunlight really my nemesis? Had things gotten *that* bad?

271 … It's not hard to slip into a daydream after a head injury. Sucking on oxygen all the time, just about every element in the universe is present and illuminated. I was dozing. This wasn't praying. The nurse was upset that I had led her to this moment in her life. She was going to take me back to the room, back to Jasper's grunting. Thankfully, Becky was coming on for a 36-hour shift. We made eye contact as she stepped out of a compact car that drove away when she waved. She knew without asking, the other nurse and I were not meant to be friends. Becky waved to us. I waved back. She came over. "Wow! I'm glad to see you're up and around." Becky offered to walk with me. The older nurse gladly handed me over. I imagined she'd go on break now. I bet she felt she deserved it. I know I said Becky wasn't a good-looking girl, but what she lacked in aesthetics she made up for in sincerity. As she leaned down to unlock my big back wheels, she whispered, "I'm sorry you had to spend a single moment with *that* woman."

272 … Becky asked me where I wanted to go. "You've been in that bed

for almost a week. I don't imagine you want to go back to your room yet."
It was just a notion at the time, but I couldn't think of a better place than
Iowa City, somewhere along the river, under a tree, in the grass. I mut-
tered, "Somewhere nice." She said, "Listen to you! Alright. I know just
the place!" We passed by a Goodwill shop and a chapel as Becky rolled
me through the halls. She opened the door to an interior arbor, a garden
between two buildings. I smelled flowers, plant life. There was running
water somewhere in the fauna. Becky positioned me in the sun. Then she
positioned me in the shade. I could reach into the sunlight or keep my
appendages to myself. Becky said, "Do you feel like talking? No? Okay,
we'll just relax here? That's a good idea. This is nice. I'm glad I ran into
you." Becky sat down on a bench surrounded by greenery. We listened to
the water fountain. I extended my arm beyond the shade, into the sunlight
and wiggled my fingers. Becky commented on my motor skills. "Your
handwriting is getting better too," she said. Better, maybe, but it wasn't
fast enough. I needed a machine to keep pace and coordinate my thoughts.

273 … Becky navigated the aisles of the bookstore. She bought us a
couple of suckers while I looked at a shelf of newspapers and magazines.
The photos, headlines and article titles were symphonies held in place
by my will to read them. When I stopped focusing the letters and words
began floating and vibrating, some of them hanging from their planes of
existence like a wet Dali painting. The words were a soup of letters and
meanings. Why I ever started writing, I'll never know. I have always been
horrified by the possibilities of choosing the incorrect arrangements. The
potential for miscommunication, the damage I could do … The fear of
making a mistake was inhibitive. Thankfully, I've made my fair share of
mistakes and talked myself into and out of corners. It makes it easier to
choose the correct words, the best phrases. Becky's sucker clicked on her
teeth. "What do you say, partner? Want to head back?" I shook my head,
"No. Good-will."

274 ... Becky guided me to the Goodwill store, but I wanted to take it from there. I wheeled through the aisles slowly. The shelves were cluttered, but I was correct in thinking I had seen a keyboard when Becky and I passed by on our way to the garden. I cleared the miscellaneous items from the rest of the typewriter. It wasn't the PowerBook I left in Iowa. This was simpler, sturdier, dumber, and heavy. I loaded it into my lap and wheeled myself to the counter. The female volunteer looked at me and the typewriter. She asked if I needed paper. I hadn't planned that far ahead. She said, "I'll get it for you." There was a stack of books next to the register with a "FREE TO A GOOD HOME" sign beside them. In the stack was Samuel Kim's "*Writing Your Memoir.*" I removed it from the stack as the volunteer returned to the counter with a partial ream of paper and a box of ribbon cartridges. She said, "You're going to need these too." She charged me for the typewriter but not the paper or the extra ribbon. "Those," she said, "are on the house."

275 ... Becky got me back to the room and into bed. She set the typewriter, paper and ribbon on the bed–table. Jasper followed Becky's movements like a hunter follows his prey until she left. I consolidated my strength and po-sitioned the typewriter ribbon on the spools and guides. I wound a piece of paper through the rollers and looked at Jasper. Jasper was watching, waiting to see what I was going to do. I positioned my hands over the keyboard and struck a key. The arm swung a decisive imprint of the letter H on the page. Jasper asked if I was going to "start ... banging ... on that thing?" I whis-pered but could not speak. "Yes."

ABOUT THE AUTHOR

Benjamin North Spencer was born in Rochester New York. He holds a BFA in Writing & Literature from the Jack Kerouac School of Disembodied Poetics at Naropa University. He has been a member of the University of Iowa Writers Workshop and the Monterey County Film Commission. He lives in Italy and California. Høney Rider is his first nøvel.

www.ingramcontent.com/pod-product-compliance
Lightning Source LLC
Chambersburg PA
CBHW03191319O626
46814CB00003BA/1225